SUFFER ASYLUM

Jack Carl Stanley

My Appreciation

The original idea to write this book came from my fiancé, Emily. She and I have watched our fair share of horror movies. There are many excellent motion pictures and stories in this category. There also exist countless terribly written scripts and books that I'm amazed ever reached the public eye.

In viewing the best this category has to offer, I found myself motivated to write a story of my own.

Further inspiration came from an occasional family tradition. On some Halloweens, my mother and I watch a classic – or sometimes not so classic – horror film. Writing my own scary tale pays homage to our sporadic ritual.

I should be clear in stating that while I am entertained by a good scare as much as the next person, I am not a terror addict. I thoroughly enjoy other genres. But nothing comes close as a medium for chills, goosebumps and the creeps.

I would like to thank Emily, my family, my friends and all of my associates – you know who you are and you've each helped me more than I can say.

Introduction

Some stories were never meant to be told.

Maybe a promise was made never to tell. Possibly someone could be damaged by information getting out and so vested interests take action to silence the author. Perhaps the exposed evil is best left untouched and unspoken.

I believe that the staff of Leiden Asylum – regardless of whatever records exist stating they have been deceased for over fifty years – won't sleep until I am stopped from releasing this exposé. And who cares if they're dead, anyways? That doesn't stop them from touching you, hurting you, ending your life . . .

"Dr." Abscheulich and his staff would stop at nothing to thwart this book. It is a story about a family, living a life not so different from others. Dysfunctional, wrong and messed up? Sure. Welcome to America. But unexpectedly, this family's world was killed and supplanted with hell.

Hell is that dark, wretched slime hiding around corners, out of sight for most and unspoken of or ignored by the rest. Hell is a blackness that envelops one in an eternal pain and finds joy in misfortune. It's been personified as different things throughout history: demons, monsters, the devil . . . But, in my case, there is a more apt word: ghosts.

Some say occasional evil spirits stay on Earth. Who knows why? I've heard that it's because these vile phantoms don't want to end up in that other place – so instead they bring a piece of it here.

Have you ever felt like someone was watching you while you sleep? You raise your head, open your eyes and one corner of your bedroom is darker than the rest? Ghosts hide in shadows and fear is their sustenance. The majority never see a ghost. A few may spot one, vaguely, at a distance and shrug it off afterwards. Fewer still may interact. And lastly, a small amount of people, usually regarded as "crazy," may actually live amongst ghosts; ghosts as real as an alive, breathing, touchable human being. This story is one of those impossible few – the alive amid the deceased; a family destroyed by living death.

Feel free to not believe me. Read my story and tell yourself, "It's not real." I couldn't care less. The only reason I have in telling anyone this story is so that Leiden Asylum can be demolished. I know that if I expose that depraved institution through this recounting, somebody out there will take proper action to rid us of the filth that resides therein.

I am writing this book in the hopes that a reader somewhere will be adequately inspired to destroy Leiden Asylum – thereby ruining Dr. Abscheulich and his wicked machine. Will you be that reader?

One could ask, "Why don't you go there and eradicate the place yourself?" Well, listen to what I impart in these pages and all will become clear. Because anyone that fully understood what I've been through would never ask me that question.

I am never going back there.

Chapter 1

Brett knew that he would be taken from his mother.

Saying that Karyn wasn't the best mom would be an understatement. She had Brett when she was 16 years old – having lied to his dad about her age.

Brett was glad that he may end up at his father's; he liked it better there anyways. His father, Mitchell, was a kind and supportive parent – the opposite of Karyn. Plus he had his little sister, Elda, to think about.

Elda was only five years old. She was still bright-eyed and excited about life. She enjoyed simple things like pretending to be animals. For her, imagination and actuality were toys to play with.

Brett looked over at Elda now; she was drawing circles with bright crayons on what appeared to be mail – completely oblivious to the fact that her mother was a drug addict.

"Yeah, I would love to live with dad," thought Brett.

With no warning, Karyn screamed, "They aren't going to take my children from me!" She turned to Brett, "You aren't going anywhere, you stupid brat!"

"Mommy!" Elda yelled, running excitedly, all smiles, toward her mother.

"Oh, get away from me," Karyn said as she pushed Elda back. "Such an annoyance." Elda, undaunted, directed her smile elsewhere and wandered off.

"Mom, no one told us they were going to take us away . . ." said Brett.

"Shut up and listen," Karyn said. "My lawyer called. That bastard said that police are coming to arrest me on ridiculous charges. Your idiot father won custody and they're taking you away. I'm getting you kids out of here. We're leaving this place for good."

Karyn ordered Brett to pack clothes. Knowing better than to argue, Brett shoved garments into trash bags. Karyn didn't own any suitcases. Brett, Elda and Karyn each had a bag of clothes.

Karyn owned virtually nothing of value. What furniture that existed was torn and ragged, clothes were faded.

Mitchell had bought the two-story house and left it with Karyn and the children – though Karyn would never admit how beneficial it was to have received a house from him.

Originally, the house was quite nice. Mitchell had gotten help from his friend Frank who owned a construction company. They had fixed the exterior and fully renovated the inside of the house. Despite the initial effort from Mitchell and Frank, Karyn hadn't kept up the place, and what was once a high-quality property was now mediocre.

It was night now; outside things were black.

Karyn said, "Brett, pick up our bags, I need to smoke." Brett threw the three black bags full of clothes over his shoulder. The bags were heavier than he could comfortably handle.

"Mom, I think these bags might break."

"Only if you carry them wrong, you fool," Karyn replied. "Lord knows, if there's a way to mess things up, you will figure it out and deliver."

Brett was used to these sorts of comments. They used to bother him, but his dad helped him. His dad didn't talk to him that way. Mitchell made him feel better about himself. Plus, Brett, at 16, had met many people – people who didn't stomp on him. People who sometimes said nice things to him and granted the occasional compliment. He figured to allow majority rule and ignore his mother's spew.

The phone rang. Karyn looked over – Brett reached for the phone. Karyn hissed, "No, you idiot!"

Suddenly blue and red lights flashed through the windows, circling around the room.

Karyn shushed her children. "They're here! You shut your mouths. We are going to go out through the basement window. Brett, get your sister down there now."

Karyn turned the radio on in the bedroom. She cranked the volume to full blast and the speakers blared loud, screechy music.

Brett, already sore from the bags, slowly made his way out of the room and headed toward the basement stairs. Elda was up past her bedtime and began whimpering. Karyn shushed Elda again. "I swear to god . . ." she said.

There was a loud knock at the door. Then silence. The family made its way down the basement stairs.

"Ms. Slinger, this is the police." Another loud knock. "Karyn Slinger, we have a warrant."

Karyn, Brett and Elda rushed into the basement. There was a sudden booming voice: "We've warned you and we're coming in!"

The front door splintered open and four policemen funneled into the house, weapons drawn.

Elda yelped but her fussing was drowned out by the music pouring from the cheap radio in the upstairs' bedroom. Brett strongly considered alerting the police but Karyn stood between Elda and him. Brett feared that his mother may do something rash and he didn't want to risk hurting Elda.

"Upstairs!" A cop yelled.

Karyn shoved Elda through a basement window. From upstairs they heard, "No one's here. Ralph and John, check out the main floor. You, come with me to check the basement!"

Brett pushed a bag through the window. He lifted the next bag upward but it caught on something and tore. Clothes spilled on the floor below. "Leave the rest and get the hell out here," Karyn snarled at Brett through gritted teeth. Brett pulled himself through the window and heard rushing footsteps nearing the basement door. Karyn climbed through the window next. "Ouch!" she said. She had cut herself on the window.

She used the sleeve of a fallen white shirt to wipe the blood and tossed it in the grass. The family emerged in the backyard and ran into the street. The police cars were parked on the reverse side of the block.

Brett could hear the sound of voices, fading in direct proportion to the growing distance.

"I should never have had children," Karyn said.

Chapter 2

Karyn and the children lived in a small town, about 50 miles away from the nearest city. The outskirts of town were surrounded by forest on all sides. Karyn knew she couldn't take her kids into town because everyone knew her. She had no plan. All she knew is that she was terrified of getting caught and her children had been her meal-ticket – she wasn't going to give them up. No children meant no lofty, monthly check for child support from Mitchell. Karyn used the majority of the cash for her own habits and benefit.

She needed to get away from where people recognize her. She knew if she could just get out of town, away from the police, she would think of something. Maybe get a lawyer and fight this. "We must arrive somewhere where no one knows us," she thought.

The only thing Karyn could think of doing was to go through the forest until they hit the nearest neighboring town – it didn't matter which one. They could stay in a hotel. Karyn had a small amount of cash; they wouldn't be able to stay in hotels for long. But Karyn didn't think long-term. She could only think of right now and the immediate future. And right now, she needed to get away from the police. So she ran toward a line of trees at the edge of a forest and yelled back to her children, "Keep up or else!"

Brett had learned by now that arguing with his logically-challenged mother was futile. He followed along, holding his sister's hand and carrying the one remaining bag over his shoulder. He wondered whose clothes were in this bag, and he considered turning back. Where would they stay? Is it safe in the forest? How would they see in the darkness? He kept these questions inside, knowing that to challenge his mother was to invite a slap across the face. Brett decided to do his part to keep his sister safe. "Besides, at the end of this, I'll be with dad and it will all be okay," Brett thought.

Elda began crying as they left the light granted by street lamps and made their way into the forest.

Karyn moved through the woodland with haste, feeling drawn toward something. She was headed in a straight line, weaving around trees. It was almost as though she were being pulled by an invisible leash, tugging at her collarbone.

Trees loomed like menacing figures. Things that held beauty in sunlight, glowered at them in the dark. They made their way through the trees, Karyn frantically panting, short-breathed from lung abuse. Brett felt branches and bushes cut at his arms. Elda was walking as fast as she could, but Karyn was getting ahead.

Suddenly a branch snagged at the bag on Brett's shoulder and tore a hole in the side. Clothes spilled out onto the forest floor. Karyn snarled back, "I knew you would screw this up! Just leave it; we need to make it to the next town."

Brett looked back as they continued pushing on. He couldn't quite see what had fallen from the bag. No time to worry. Elda kept crying.

They continued on through the forest. It was damp and numbingly chilly. Their eyelids were heavy and their feet ached. On and on, through sunless woods and dirt.

They walked for what seemed like hours. Elda had stopped crying and Brett gave her a piggyback ride to help her keep up.

Brett had his attention on his mother. She seemed to know where she was going. "How could that be possible?" Brett thought. They were in jet-black woods, deeper than any of them had ever been before. He worried about Elda.

Brett squinted ahead. Despite the utter darkness, he thought he could make out some fog ahead.

He was getting tired. It was already late and he had had judo practice earlier that day. He was a blue belt. He was told that he could have been a black belt by now, had his mother taken him to tournaments. But on the weekends he spent at his mother's, she never drove him to any competitions. Brett was sore from being thrown around during class for two hours that day.

Maybe it was the tiredness but Brett thought he was seeing the fog form into a shape. Yes, through the black he saw mist rising up. It began twisting upward and forming the appearance of a human figure. The figure began turning toward the family. Just when Brett almost made out its face -

"Brett! Stop daydreaming and hurry up! I think I see a house we can stay at tonight," yelled Karyn. Brett snapped his view to his mother. "It looks like there's some sort of mansion ahead."

Brett looked back to the fog. The figure was completely gone. "I must just be tired," thought Brett.

The family made its way through the darkness and as they broke through the tree line Brett made out a large property. There was a fifteen-foot high metal fence, with spikes at the top all pointed inward. The fence was not meant to keep trespassers out; it was designed to keep residents in. Through the fence he saw a large building. It looked like an abandoned hospital. Or worse, a dilapidated prison.

The family walked across an overgrown field toward the fence. "We can stay inside this place for the night," Karyn said.

They arrived at the fence, panting and cold. There was no way in. Elda lay down in the grass. Karyn and Brett searched around the fence, looking for an entrance. They made it to what appeared to be the main gate. It was chained shut. Thick, rusted, chain-linked and padlocked in several places. Karyn shook the gate, screamed in frustration and collapsed. Elda had had her share of crying; Karyn felt it was her turn now. They had already made their way through miles of forest and it was well past midnight. Each of them was tired, cold and supposed to be sleeping.

Elda was lying in the grass, passed out. Brett looked around. They couldn't get over the barrier. Not only was the fifteen feet of fence unclimbable, they would be stabbed should they reach the top.

Brett put his hand on his mother's shoulder and she instantly flinched. "Get off of me; sympathy won't get us a warm bed tonight."

She climbed up and told Brett to wake his sister. They would have to keep moving on.

But out of nowhere, a light danced over them.

A person opened the main door to the building and walked out. It appeared he was carrying a lantern.

His face shone in the darkness. The person looked familiar to Brett. He couldn't quite place it.

They walked closer, down the path toward the gate where the family stood outside. It was a man with a thin, sharp face. He had round glasses, grey-black hair and looked to be about fifty. He was wearing a white overcoat and appeared to be a doctor. He looked down his sharp nose at them, firelight flickering off his dark-blue eyes. The family stared.

"Welcome to Leiden Asylum, Karyn," the man said. "We've been expecting you."

Chapter 3

The man began unlocking the gate. Karyn looked surprised, "How do you know who I am? What do you mean you're expecting me?" Her voice was quavering.

Meanwhile, Elda was standing behind Brett, holding his hand and shivering in fear. Usually Elda would effusively greet people, even strangers; this was a strange reaction on her part.

"Please excuse me, my name is Dr. Abscheulich." His voice sounded foreign, possibly German. Like one of those old-fashioned psychiatrists you see in the movies. "You applied for an assistant nurse position here. Karyn Aargon Slinger. You sent in a resume and a cover letter, and there's a small photo of you that comes with your email. You also mentioned you had two children in your cover letter. It is quite a surprise to see you all here, at this time of night. But when you last spoke to my staff, they said you informed them that you would be coming down soon to get to work. And so, we've been expecting you. We haven't received many applicants and you've already completed most of our hiring process."

Karyn was biting her lip, attempting to concentrate as the doctor spoke. "Do I remember him?" she thought. "I have sent out a lot of resumes – I have to keep receiving unemployment." As a result of her addictions, her memory had been failing her for some time. It was quite possible that she had applied for a job here. She had applied everywhere within a twenty-five-mile radius of her house. Never actually showing up for job interviews; just doing the minimum requirements to keep her checks coming in. It seemed as though the doctor was telling the truth. Besides, how else would he know these personal things about her?

Who was Karyn to argue? It was nearly the middle of the night and her family needed food and shelter. Better yet, it was quite unlikely that the police would check an asylum for her and her children, especially one in the middle of nowhere. Karyn decided that it was more likely than not that she had indeed applied for a position here.

Karyn responded, "Yes, of course I applied and I do wish to be a nurse here. This job includes room and board, right?" Hoping for the best.

"Why yes," replied Dr. Abscheulich. "Forgive me for asking, but have you no recollection of speaking with Leiden Asylum? You look and sound as though your concourse with us evacuated your memory."

"No, no, no, no. I remember everything. And I'm sorry for showing up like this; we were planning on arriving much earlier today but our car broke down several miles from here. I'm afraid we've been walking for hours," lied Karyn.

Brett was not surprised by this. His mother had always said whatever would get her what she wanted. Brett knew she was being false – she had no memory of applying here. And frankly, after years of deceit and nonexistent parenting, Brett was inclined to believe this strange doctor more than his "mother." But still . . . Why did the doctor look so familiar?

Dr. Abscheulich had finished unlocking the gate at this point and had it open. "I'm sorry to hear that. I'm glad your legs carried you to our door. We are in need of another nurse. Consider yourself hired. Now, follow me, let's fill your hollow stomachs."

As they headed down the path toward the front door of the asylum, a huge man hulked out from inside. He appeared to be hooded. The shadows covered his face. You could see his chest slowly heaving up and down, in steady, even breaths. Almost like he was timing them exactly, methodically.

Brett broke off his view from the brawny beast and looked at the windows. "Strange," he thought, "several lights are on now." When they walked up several minutes ago, the place looked abandoned and dark. Now it appeared to be an occupied, functional mental hospital. He could see patient rooms, covered windows – it *was* an asylum. "Maybe I'm just tired," he thought, again.

The doctor motioned for the family to walk inside. He lingered behind for a moment outside to whisper to the brute at the door.

The family couldn't hear, but the doctor said, "Lock the gate."

Chapter 4

As the family entered the main lobby, twenty staff stood waiting in a semi-circle. They all had blank smiles.

Brett shuddered. Elda remained behind him, still clutching his hand; her typical jovial demeanor nonexistent.

Karyn beamed. "Yeah, there's no way we will be found here," she thought. She smiled, feeling safe for the first time in hours.

The staff all had glazed-over eyes and there was something menacing in the way their lips curved upwards on their face. False smiles.

Dr. Abscheulich walked in front of the staff and introduced them. There were nurses and orderlies. They all had white uniforms. The women wore those old-fashioned hats. It appeared that the outfits for the nurses were designed by a sexist man, bottoms too high and tops too low. All of the nurses appeared young and pretty. Only one looked to be over forty. She had brown hair and pure black eyes. Her skin was wrinkled and she had thin, pale pink lips. For some reason, Brett's gaze lingered on her.

"Karyn, Brett, young Elda," announced Dr. Abscheulich, "this is the staff of Leiden Asylum. You will meet each person in their own time. For now, I will introduce you to our head nurse, Nurse Rieck."

The woman Brett had stared at stepped forward. Her motions were jerky and fast. It looked as though she was in line one moment and two feet ahead the next. She maintained the same, unflinching smile.

Actually, since first looking at the staff, none had changed their facial expression.

"Nurse Rieck is my right hand," continued Dr. Abscheulich. "There is no way I could keep the hundred and thirty-two patients we have here in check without her."

Karyn walked forward to shake Nurse Rieck's hand. The nurse met her grip in that same rapid, twitching motion. They shook hands and Karyn said, "Good to meet you."

Nurse Rieck responded in a screechy voice, sounding as one may imagine dust sounds. "Welcome. I look forward to working with you, Karyn." Nurse Rieck jerked her head to Brett. Still smiling that forced smile, a smile that appeared to have been tattooed on her face and maintained regardless of her will, she stared into Brett's eyes, as though she were attempting to enter his mind – an unexpected guest into his personal thoughts. "And so this is Brett," she said, maintaining her gaze longer than what could be considered comfortable.

"And sweet Elda," she said as she was suddenly found kneeling and several feet closer than she had been a moment before. Elda cringed and squeezed her brother's hand tighter. "You're going to have a *terribly* good time here . . ." Elda whimpered.

"I must retire," said Dr. Abscheulich, "so, I bid you all goodnight." He slid off into the shadows of a nearby hallway, looking at the family the entire way, until the caverns on his face were hidden in non-light.

"I will show you to your room," Nurse Rieck hissed at the family.

Brett knew something was definitely wrong – beyond creepy. "Why have I never heard of this place?" he thought. "What is wrong with these people?"

Two burly attendants appeared behind the family to help guide them. The nurse led the family through the hall. The walls were freshly painted. There were barred windows on the doors they passed.

Brett was glancing in the windows. He could see people moving inside some of the rooms, but they were walking too fast to observe in detail. The lights were off inside some of the rooms but there were definitely people in there – patients. Brett panned his head from right to left and saw eyes glaring at him from one of the rooms. The face had poorly done stitches across various sections and the skin appeared grey. It was a man with gapped, crooked, yellow teeth and an evil smile. He was staring at Brett. His head was massive. The man began pulling at one of his stitches and Brett saw blood begin streaming down his face and then he was cut off from view. The family had walked too far and turned a corner.

"Stop!" yelled Brett. Everyone ceased walking. "There's a man back there – he was tearing at stitches on his face. And . . . and . . . bleeding. What the he—"

Nurse Rieck cut in, "Where did you see this?"

Brett rushed back around the corner and pointed. He pointed at the exact space on the wall where there should have been a door. Brett looked frantically up and down the hall – there were no doors. Just long, white, bare walls. Brett was speechless.

Nurse Rieck said, "There, there Brett. I know you must just be tired. This isn't the time for jokes though. We really should be getting you all to bed."

Brett was stunned. He knew what he had seen.

Karyn said, "Oh knock it off Brett, it's late. We don't have time for your games."

"No use arguing with her," Brett thought. "I learned that long ago." Brett forced a nod. He had to get his family out of here.

"Oh you silly boy," said Nurse Rieck. "Your humor is absolutely *deadly.*"

Chapter 5

The family was now in a room, alone.

It was like a furnished cell.

There was a bathroom and a half wall that divided Karyn's bed from Brett's and Elda's.

There were two credenzas with mirrors, one on each side of the room. There were three dressers. All of these items appeared to be brand new but had an old-fashioned look.

Karyn was sprawled and snoring in her bed. Elda was also asleep, in a separate bed. Now Brett was the only one awake. The room was dark but a small amount of yellow light came in underneath the door from the hallway. Brett walked to the window and attempted to open it. There were bars and a metal grate over the window. There was no way to get it open. It was built into the structure of the building.

Brett looked out the window. It was the middle of the night. The entire complex was surrounded by woods – the trees lining the exterior seemed to bar them even further, acting as a second fence. This room was like being locked in a jail, within a jail, within a jail. Not only that, they were miles from anywhere. "Not getting out this window," Brett thought. He looked over at Elda.

Shadows flickered in the light behind him. Brett spun around to view the door. Nothing there. He held his sight there for a moment, just to make sure.

He looked back out the window and there was that fog again. And once more, it was forming a shape. Light flickered behind him again.

Brett looked back at the door and saw nothing. This time he walked to the door. He reached it and looked out into the hallway. There he saw it, the massive stitched man grinning right at him. Brett's heart stopped. This guy must be three hundred pounds and was over six feet tall. He was in a strait jacket but one arm was torn out. In it, a red shard of glass. There was blood on his face from where he had pulled at his stitches. It was clear that this man was a patient.

The monster was giggling and pointing at something. Brett followed the direction indicated by the finger and saw a woman. She had greasy, ratty, dark brown hair. Blood was smeared across the floor. She was breathing heavily.

The brute shoved the glass between his teeth, lumbered over to the woman on the floor and lifted her clear into the air with his one arm – like she was a stuffed animal. The woman screamed. Brett was frantically attempting to open the door but it was locked from the outside. Brett pounded on the door and yelled, "Knock it off! Leave her alone!"

Brett watched in horror as the psychotic smashed the woman's head against the wall; it appeared he silenced her for good. A large red patch was left behind on the wall. He dropped her like a sack on the floor.

Karyn, hearing Brett's commotion, jerked awake. "What the hell is going on?"

Brett looked toward his mother just as the man plunged the glass toward the deceased woman's eye. Brett was stone white and couldn't believe he had just witnessed a murder. In a hushed, frantic voice, he told his mother to come to the door.

She struggled up, limped over in a tired stupor and hit Brett on the side of the head. He looked at her and pointed into the hallway. Karyn looked. "What, Brett? There's nothing there but walls, a ceiling and a floor."

Brett looked out as well. There was no trace of anything.

He tried the door. It opened.

Brett looked up and down the hallway. No one was there. No blood. No glass. Not a thing in sight.

"Mom, I know what I saw," Brett asserted. "This place is beyond messed up. I just saw a woman get murdered. We need to call the -"

"What? The police?" Karyn sneered sharply. "You stupid teenager. I'll be put in jail and you'll end up at your deadbeat father's. I've had enough of your lies."

Brett was fed up and had had enough. "Shut up, you addict!" yelled Brett. Karyn's mouth dropped, the combination of sleep-deprivation and never being talked to in this way leaving her without words. "I know what I saw. This place is wrong and I will not sit here, risking my sister's life, so that you can escape justice. We're not going down with you. We're out of here."

Karyn threw a punch at Brett but this time he used some light judo to defend himself. Karyn fell lightly into a wall but over-exaggerated the nonexistent pain.

Mitchell had thoroughly indoctrinated Brett never to attack women. Brett remembered one of the many long conversations that he had with his father on the subject. "Listen, Brett," Mitchell explained. "I know your mom abuses you and it's completely not okay. I promise I will gain custody and you won't have to deal with it anymore. I have made it known to the police and it's come up in our court case. But you can't hurt her. Sure, defend yourself, but never hit a woman. You know martial arts and she doesn't. Plus most of her actions are motivated by drugs, alcohol and sins. When she gets like that, just get away from her until she calms down. I promise you won't have to deal with it forever, but a real man never hits a woman." The talk echoed in Brett's mind as he walked over to his sister's bed and woke her up – she had somehow slept through all the noise. "I was defending myself," he told himself.

Karyn crawled into the hall and yelled, "Help! I'm being attacked!" Mysteriously, Dr. Abscheulich and Nurse Rieck immediately appeared, as though they were hovering behind the nearest corner.

Nurse Rieck removed a syringe from her pocket with a dexterity that proved prior experience and Dr. Abscheulich said, "Brett, it appears you're attacking your mother. If you don't stop immediately, we will be forced to restrain you."

Brett calmed himself, looked squarely at the doctor and said, "Sir, my mother is not being attacked. I just witnessed someone in the hall being murdered. There was this man -"

"You saw no such thing!" cut in Karyn. "He's lying, Doctor. He always lies!"

Brett's face turned hot with anger and he continued, "There was this man that was beating a woman. There was blood and he was killing her." Karyn persisted in trying to interrupt but Brett pressed on. "He must have cleaned up and carried her off with speed. I know what I saw. It was the same guy that I saw when we were walking through the hallway earlier."

"You mean the man you saw through a window, in a windowless passage?" Nurse Rieck inquired sarcastically. Brett noticed two large men were now standing in the doorway, wearing white scrubs.

Brett inched closer to his sister. He kept his vision and peripheral on all present.

"I don't need anyone here to believe me, I know what I saw. This place is unsafe and my sister and I will now be leaving," Brett said and put his hand on Elda.

Karyn screamed, "Leave my little girl alone!" Elda pulled Brett's hand close and squeezed. Karyn and the two large orderlies walked toward Brett.

Brett picked up Elda and began walking to the door. Karyn again attempted to slap Brett and he quickly dodged her slow, flailing motion.

The two men now blocked Brett's path. He set Elda down and set himself in a standard judo fighting stance. The man on the left reached toward Brett. Brett nimbly flipped the man onto his back. One of the beauties of judo is that you use the opponent's strength and size against them: the bigger they are, the harder they fall. The man to Brett's right swung his fist in an attempt to punch Brett's face; Brett gripped his arm on the wrist and above the elbow and threw the man several feet into a wall.

Brett turned to grab his sister again and felt a stabbing prick in the back of his arm. Nurse Rieck injected him with something. He was amazed he hadn't noticed her. Immediately, Brett felt a cloud of dizziness fall over him. The room spun and he toppled over. Everything went black. Brett was out.

Chapter 6

Mitchell Slinger had persistently worked at gaining full custody of his children and, due to lawyers and court delays, the whole thing had taken years.

Thankfully, he had finally been able to prove to the court and police that Karyn had been abusing illegal substances.

He had hired a private investigator and gotten video and photographic evidence. Karyn was then ordered by a judge to do drug testing and the results were resoundingly positive.

She was unfit to be a mother. Justice had finally shown through.

Mitchell stood with his lawyer at the police station. He had the written consent of the judge. Two officers were to take him to Karyn's house and ensure the whole thing went smoothly. And additionally, they had a warrant for Karyn's arrest.

The policemen entered their vehicle. Mitchell climbed in the back and they drove toward Karyn's house.

On the drive there, Mitchell called the house and there was no answer. He was afraid that Karyn would run. He leaned forward and told the officers, "I just called the house and no one picked up. Knowing Karyn, I'm worried she may try to run off with the children."

The driver nodded in response and switched the police lights on. Mitchell clenched his fist and frantically dialed Karyn's house again. The car sped down the road, drivers swerving to the roadside out of a fear they'd be arrested should they violate traffic laws – as though the police would stop their rush to pull over a bystander.

They arrived at the house and the officers got out of the car. Mitchell did as well but was stopped. "Sir, stay by the car. We'll handle this." Mitchell attempted to argue but was interrupted with, "Stay."

The officers went to the front door to knock. Mitchell looked at the house and wondered if Karyn would have the audacity to run from the police. He stared hawk-like at all visible windows and the front door.

Music suddenly could be heard playing inside the house. "Ms. Slinger, this is the police. Karyn Slinger, we have a warrant," one of the officers said loudly after knocking.

Another police car arrived and two more officers joined the others at the front door.

"This is taking too long," Mitchell thought. "Officers!" he yelled, "She must be trying to escape." One of the officers nodded in response and then said, "We've warned you and we're coming in!" He kicked down the door.

Mitchell said, "Screw this," under his breath and ran in the house.

"Upstairs!" A cop yelled.

Mitchell stayed on the main floor and checked the living room and the kitchen. He then walked to the basement stairs, opened the door and rushed down the stairs. He saw a torn garbage bag with clothes piled all over. The basement window was open. Mitchell shouted for the police and ran over to the window. He looked out and saw a pitch-black backyard.

On the ground outside the window was a bloodied white shirt.

No children in sight.

Chapter 7

Brett awoke in a haze. The room appeared grey and his head spun. There was a piercing pain in his brain. He attempted to strain his eyes to make the fuzziness dissipate but to no avail. At first Brett thought he was in his bedroom at home and tried to locate a landmark of some sort, but his sight failed him.

He shut his eyes tightly. A few minutes passed before Brett could focus his eyes and he began to make out the room. He was in a padded cell, lying on a bed. Straps lay open by his wrists and ankles. It all came back to him. He was at Leiden Asylum. He had witnessed a murder. He had been drugged.

Brett's thoughts drifted to a previous memory. He was at Karyn's house with Elda. It was around noon on a weekend day. Karyn was passed out on the couch, while Elda played in the backyard. Brett and Elda had been up for hours and he had cooked her breakfast.

This behavior was typical – Brett caring for his sister as Karyn lazed, hungover. Brett was on the phone with a girl from school, Lillian. "So, what are you up to today, Lilly?" he asked, keeping an eye on Elda who was playing with dolls in the grass.

"Just sitting around," she responded. "Do you want to hang out?"

Suddenly Karyn came up from behind Brett and slapped him on the back of the head. "Where's my breakfast?" she demanded.

"I'll call you back, Lilly," Brett said and quickly ended the call. "You were sleeping, I thought -" he began.

"Knock off the excuses," Karyn interrupted, "and make me some food. Now!"

Brett's attention snapped back to the present. He slowly sat up in the bed. A picture of Lillian flashed in his mind. She was beautiful – another reason for him to get out of this place!

The room was dimly lit with a flickering light. His head hurt terribly, so Brett took a moment to rest it in his hand, clenching his eyes shut.

He re-opened them and made out a shadow in the corner of his room near the door. "Who's there?" said Brett. The figure slid over the floor toward him and he quickly saw it was Nurse Rieck.

"Hello, boy," she snarled. "Another outburst from you and you'll find yourself in solitary confinement. Don't think we won't forcibly commit you."

Brett stared. Years of experience with his mother had taught him how to recognize a crazy person. He knew they couldn't be reasoned with.

"Well?" she said, a slight smile ever-present on her face and blank eyes glaring with evil.

"Yes, ma'am."

"Good," she replied. "Now, it's lunch time. Come to the cafeteria."

Brett stood up, restraining the urge to show his discomfort. He then noticed that he was in a sort of hospital gown. He wondered why he was wearing patient's clothing. He saw his clothes lying on the floor. Nurse Rieck turned her back and he quickly threw them on.

Nurse Rieck then knocked on the door. A burly guard unlocked the door from the outside. "So, I was locked in," Brett thought.

Nurse Rieck seemed to float when she walked but Brett could see her feet moving. He followed her down the hallway. She looked back at him as she moved, never breaking her gaze. Brett felt uncomfortable. "Why is she staring at me?" he thought. They turned a corner; she continued to peer at him.

Brett broke the silence with chatter. "So, how long have you worked here?"

Nurse Rieck blinked. "Most of my life. But sorry, my dear, I have no liking for you and zero interest in conversing. Now hurry, your family is waiting." Brett frowned and looked away.

They entered a cafeteria. Elda spotted Brett and ran over. "Bro bro!" She hugged him. He was glad to see that she was safe. Karyn glared at him.

Brett sat down at the table for breakfast. He looked around the room. This appeared to be a dining hall. Brett then realized it was cafeteria-style serving, self-serve, so he stood up and grabbed himself a tray. Elda followed him.

Brett felt as though every person in the room was staring at him. He concentrated on the food that was being offered. It appeared to be container after container of grey mush. He scooped himself some slime and made his way back to the table. Yes, the asylum inhabitants were looking at him from their tables. On their faces were either ferocious glowers or stabbing eyes and a false smile. Regardless of facial expressions, Brett perceived a pungent urge to harm emanating from the surrounding personages.

He sat. Elda joined him, pressed snugly on his side. Karyn was across from him, chatting with a nurse on her right. "After lunch, Karyn, we will continue with your orientation."

Brett thought to himself, "This place is more of a prison than a hospital." He half expected to see snipers placed in towers throughout the grounds.

Brett noticed a solitary woman beyond the eating area. The lone woman was standing, faced toward Brett. She was a patient, looking directly at him. She had blonde hair, blue eyes and a pretty face. She looked like she was in her twenties. She was looking directly at Brett but her expression was kind. She looked familiar.

Karyn slammed her hand on the table. "I asked you something, you insolent boy!" she snarled. "Who are you staring at?" Brett was startled by the outburst which had taken his attention. He returned his gaze to the familiar woman and pointed.

She was gone.

Chapter 8

Karyn had blonde hair and sharp, blue eyes. Drug use had caused excessive wrinkles for someone in their 30s and she had deep bags under her eyes.

Karyn was actually a pretty woman. But self-inflicted abuse had dirtied her appearance. Karyn had insisted on surgical enhancements for herself while with Mitchell, so he paid for them.

She was about 5' 6" and was average weight. Cosmetic surgery had made her more curvaceous and young-looking, but dark circles under her eyes betrayed her. Her hair was naturally dirty blonde but she used platinum blonde hair dye. Though beautiful, she would be more so had she stifled her immoral urges.

She had met Mitchell sixteen years ago. She'd told him she was twenty at the time but in actuality she had been sixteen years old. She had false identification made up that allowed her to fool authorities and others around her.

Mitchell and Karyn met through a mutual friend. Karyn knew Mitchell had money and he was overwhelmed with attraction toward her. Their relationship started wonderfully and it seemed they were truly in love. The rush of dates and wedding planning took attention away from ominous indicators.

They were married and pregnant with Brett within their first year together. Things rapidly fell downhill after the wedding. Karyn's undisclosed drug use was a factor in their severance.

Mitchell felt that Karyn had pretended to be someone other than her true self to trick him into marriage. He soon after discovered hidden secrets on her part – amongst them being that Karyn had fallen into the arms of several other men.

Things ended when Brett was a small child – long before Elda was born. The fact that Karyn had cheated on Mitchell caused their first separation. Despite the betrayal, Mitchell continued to care about Karyn and provided for her.

Several years after their initial break up, Karyn and Mitchell temporarily made up. The reparation resulted in Elda but ended the same way as the prior attempt at a partnership.

Karyn now stood dressed in a nurse's uniform and was tasked with standing behind a window dispensing pills to the patients. She looked very pleased with her new assignment. There was a line of staring patients, awaiting their stupor-inducing substances. Karyn methodically provided each one with a paper cup filled with an assortment of tablets.

Brett watched from a distance. Elda was playing nearby. She had found some papers and was enjoying herself, crumpling them into balls.

There was a man in a patient's robe strolling around nearby. He had thin hair and was hunched over, looking at the floor. The man looked deflated and his eyes were glazed over. Brett noticed a scar near the top of his forehead.

Worried that the man would interact with his sister, Brett joined her and they pretended the paper orbs were various people and animals. Due to their large gap in age and their mother's poor parenting abilities, Brett and Elda actually got along better than most brothers and sisters. Brett did more to raise Elda than Karyn did.

Brett thought about the countless times that Karyn lay on the couch or in her room, hungover or worse, completely neglecting Elda and him.

Karyn had finished dispensing pills. "Here, take these," a nurse said as she handed Karyn three large pills. Karyn didn't ask but instead downed the capsules.

The nurse looked toward Brett. In an effort to avoid being drugged again Brett stood up and told Elda, "Come on, let's go explore."

Elda squealed in joy and abandoned her paper spheres.

The walls in the institution were all solid white with old-fashioned tile floors. The ceilings were white square panels. Most of the doors were made of metal but some of the doors leading to staff offices looked like solid oak. Brett noticed occasional ventilation covers on the bottom of walls, resting about a foot above the floor. "That's a strange place for vents," he thought. Though everything looked fairly recently painted and installed, the building still seemed old somehow.

Brett and Elda turned down the nearest hallway. A few feet away, Brett saw double doors labeled "SURGERY." Brett led Elda in that direction. As he approached he heard screaming. He pushed through the doors. "Stay close," he told his sister.

"Why there yelling?" Elda inquired.

"Don't worry," Brett replied. "They're just playing."

He eased his way down the hall. There was a doorway on his right. Brett peeked in. The door was open and the room was empty. There was a surgical table and supplies. The room smelled horrid and looked unclean.

In the room was a window to the outside. Brett walked over to it and looked out. It was foggy outside. He could make out the fence past the grass. He then noticed a shape. It was that ghostly figure again. Brett stared. It reminded him of someone . . .

A noise nearby cut off his gaze. Elda had squealed and pointed at the floor. Brett looked and saw a trail that seemed eerily similar to blood. He knew that it wasn't safe to bring his sister here but he wanted to find the source of the bellows – it had sounded as though someone were in danger.

The sounds had stopped. The silence was almost as bad as the screaming had been.

Brett and Elda left the room and continued down the hallway and reached another door. This one was shut. There was a window. Brett quickly peered in. Inside he saw a terrible sight!

A doctor was standing over a man. The man appeared unconscious. The doctor held two large spike-like objects in his hand and was piercing them into the man's exposed brain. Two nurses stood nearby, apparently to provide the doctor with needed instruments. He recognized the nurses from when the staff were introduced last night – one of them was a redhead and the other was a short brunette. Under different circumstances, they could be considered good-looking.

There was blood trickling down the front and sides of the patient's head. Brett was dumbfounded and speechless. He had never seen such a gruesome sight in real life. The doctor was a thin, balding man with glasses.

The scene was grotesque and the fact that everyone (excepting the patient of course) was smiling made matters even worse. Brett was no surgeon, but there appeared to be too much blood loss.

Elda spoke out, "What you see, bro bro?"

Hearing her words, the doctor and nurses turned their heads and looked right at Brett!

Chapter 9

The cops searched the house for two hours, even closing off the block with police tape. Mitchell stood outside, frustrated that they were spending so much time in the house. It was obvious the kids weren't there. Karyn had taken them.

It was very late at night and Karyn's car was still parked outside the house. Mitchell walked up to the lead detective outside the house. Though it legally takes twenty-four hours for people to be classified as missing persons, Mitchell had connections in the community and Karyn already had a criminal record.

The blood on the shirt had everyone worried. The police had sent it in for testing to determine whose blood it was.

"Well, any luck?" asked Mitchell.

"Obviously we haven't found them if that's what you're asking," stated the detective. "Evidently they made their way out of the basement window and, judging by the abandoned clothing, they were in a hurry. Most likely escaping just as we arrived. I have some police searching nearby properties. I'm personally calling all hotels nearby tonight. It's late; they're probably holed up somewhere close. We are launching search dogs in the morning. We're a little undermanned due to the time of night, but we're canvassing the neighborhood the best we can."

"Understood, Detective."

"Thank you. The name's Ernest; just call me Ernest."

They exchanged numbers and Mitchell decided to continue a search on his own. He walked over to the downstairs window. He was standing in the backyard and crouched down. He couldn't see any footprints in the dirt.

Dark thoughts raced through his mind. Are his children hurt? Are they in danger? What if Karyn had done the unthinkable? "Stop," Mitchell told himself, "these thoughts aren't helping anything."

He glanced across the backyard. He couldn't see any obvious traces of where they went.

Knowing Karyn, she probably hadn't thought this out at all. Most likely she just started running.

Mitchell walked to the back of the backyard and looked past the fence. There was a street, several nearby houses and, of course, the forest.

He spent the next several minutes walking past houses, looking for any clues as to their location. With a five-year-old, and all on foot, it isn't likely they went too far. He circled back to the backyard and then headed in the opposite direction for a while. House after house, all blacked out due to the fact it was the middle of the night. No luck.

Mitchell stood in the backyard again and looked out. A crazy thought entered his mind. "Maybe she took them into the forest?" It was worth a shot.

He exited the backyard, crossed the street and entered the forest directly across from Karyn's house. It was black. Mitchell used the flashlight on his phone. He could see now, but barely. The forest floor was covered with leaves and foliage. There was no exposed dirt so it was hard to find footprints. Plus Mitchell wasn't a professional tracker.

Mitchell spent a few minutes in the cold forest to no avail. Then his phone rang. It was Detective Ernest. Ernest told Mitchell that Karyn's lawyer had informed her that she was to be arrested and that Mitchell had gained full custody. Per the lawyer, this had caused a major upset and he wasn't surprised when he heard the kids were missing.

Mitchell ended the call and returned to the backyard. Out of the short list of possible places Karyn ran off to, Mitchell still felt the forest shouldn't be ruled out. She would have been panicked and she doesn't have any friends nearby. She couldn't have run toward a hotel because she knew the police were looking for her.

Mitchell decided to take it upon himself to check with the neighbors. It was now the middle of the night. He approached the first door and knocked. No response. Then he rang the doorbell. A light clicked on. The door burst open. "What?!" There was an older woman and she looked very alarmed. In her right hand, she held a kitchen knife.

After checking in with four houses, with no success, Mitchell decided against continuing his door-to-door search at this time of night. He also doubted that Karyn went to a neighbor's home.

As each minute passed, Mitchell's worry grew. He continued to push negative impressions from his mind. It was a couple hours to dawn now. Mitchell told himself, "They're sleeping safely somewhere right now."

Mitchell saw Detective Ernest standing near his squad car. It looked like the police were clearing out. Mitchell jogged over. "You heading out?" he asked.

"Yeah, we're going to get a little shut eye and continue the search in the morning," Ernest responded.

"Alright," said Mitchell. "I looked around and I think there's a chance they headed into the forest."

"Really?" replied Ernest. "That sounds ridiculous. Why would they head to the forest? It's far more likely she went to a hotel or caught a bus out of town."

"Yeah, but -" started Mitchell.

"What are you, a detective now?" Ernest cut in. "Just let us do our investigation."

Mitchell nodded in response. Detective Ernest looked at Mitchell for a moment with a raised eyebrow, then sighed. "Listen, there are no signs of forced entry or evidence that anything bad has happened. By all indications, Karyn has simply taken them elsewhere. You've no need to worry. It is most likely that one of them cut themselves on the window while leaving. All fingers point to Karyn. We will find them and she will be dealt with."

Mitchell looked to the ground and frowned. "They're safe," the detective finished. Mitchell thanked him and called a cab. He decided to rest for a couple hours and then join the morning search party. Mitchell repeated the detective's words, "They're safe," in his mind.

How very wrong Detective Ernest was.

Chapter 10

The doctor rushed to the door and opened it with a rough motion. Brett backed up in the hall and stood in front of Elda, as though to shield her.

"You cannot be here," the doctor forcefully told them. Elda started crying.

"We heard screaming," explained Brett. "Is everything okay? Because by the look and sound of it, you're killing him."

"Though I have neither need nor obligation to inform you, I'm performing a lobotomy of sorts," the doctor explained. "My name is Dr. Schlagen and I am a surgeon here. These incisions are vital. But you wouldn't understand. Your age and lack of any valuable training prohibits comprehension. We are making history and designing future's path. Transcending the boundaries of brain and mind. The grey matter that oversees all."

During his short speech, the doctor didn't blink. Brett grabbed Elda's hand. "You're scaring her, you weirdo," stated Brett. "And whatever you're doing to that man can't be helping him."

"Hush, boy," the doctor hissed. "Your impudence and closed-minded blindness will end you up unaccompanied."

Brett glared and turned to exit. "Jesus!" he yelled. Inches from his face stood Dr. Abscheulich.

"Well, Mr. Slinger," Dr. Abscheulich began. "Wandering, are we?"

"We were just leaving," Brett replied.

"I'll join you," said Dr. Abscheulich.

Elda had stopped sobbing and pulled at Brett's hand. "We go now?" she inquired, as she looked up. "Scary man," pointing directly at Dr. Abscheulich.

Dr. Schlagen returned to his surgical room and shut the door. A lock clicked.

Brett followed Dr. Abscheulich down the hallway. "Brett, I will take you to my office. Elda will join Karyn." They opened the double doors and re-entered the pill dispensary room.

Karyn was laughing with a nurse. She looked over and frowned at the sight of her children. Elda yelled, "Momma!" and ran over to Karyn.

"This way, Mr. Slinger," Dr. Abscheulich commanded. He headed up a nearby staircase. At the landing there was a large iron door. Brett trailed behind the doctor. Dr. Abscheulich removed a large set of heavy keys and unlocked the door. There were two locks, a separate key for each.

Brett felt a cold chill and the urge to look behind him. He did so and Nurse Rieck glared at him from the bottom of the stairs. She held something in her hand – it looked like a loaded syringe.

Brett heard the second lock disengage. He walked behind the doctor into an office. It was a grand workplace. There was a large fireplace with a marble mantel. The fire was lit and in front of it were two chairs and a chaise longue. The motif was deep red cherry wood. There was an elegant carpet and even a grizzly bear rug.

Brett's inspection of the room was interrupted by Dr. Abscheulich's snake-like voice. "I will attempt to impart to you the necessity of this institution. Come now, sit."

The doctor sat at an imposing desk and indicated a seat in front of it. Brett walked over and sat. The doctor lifted the edge of his mouth slightly and continued. "Not only does Leiden Asylum see to society's mentally deranged, it researches cutting-edge remedies for mental ailments. We are trusted by important individuals, who shall not be named, to resolve the psychotic. I have found that impressions made upon the brain affects all behavior. Lacerations, electricity, insulin, flashing lights, medications . . . Even simple commodities like water or air can be used to change people."

"So, you're experimenting here?" Brett queried.

"No," the doctor replied with mild irritation in his voice, "experimentation suggests a lack of certainty as to outcome. No, boy, our research is proven. We are simply perfecting our already workable techniques. By snipping small, precise sections of the brain, I can make the most violent of psychopaths docile. We can reduce the uncontrollable to tame. I have unlocked the recalcitrance of man."

Brett was bored by the conversation and wondered how Elda was doing. He needed to get them both out of this hellhole. Brett doubted that Karyn would want to leave.

"Which brings me to you, Brett," continued the doctor. "You have severe untreated mental issues. Mood disorders that need to be addressed."

Brett scowled at the doctor, disagreeing with everything he said.

The doctor continued, "So, without further delay, let us begin your treatment."

Chapter 11

Elda played near her mother. She had empty paper cups and was using a pen to draw them into people. "This one's you mommy," Elda said as she proudly held up an inked cup.

Karyn ignored her and continued talking with a fellow nurse. "Dr. Abscheulich said that he believes that your son is in need of therapy, medication and possibly psycho-surgery," uttered the nurse.

"You're telling me," answered Karyn. "Brett is nothing but trouble. I would feel completely honored to have the doctor fix him. God knows I've failed."

Elda was getting bored and tugged at her mother's leg. "Oh, go play somewhere!" Karyn snapped. Elda frowned, stood up and wandered over to the nearest wall. She started drawing on it.

Karyn took no notice and continued chatting.

Up the nearby staircase Brett exited the doctor's office. "No," he said, "I'm not a patient here and I won't let you 'treat' me." Dr. Abscheulich followed as Brett rushed down the stairs.

"Mom," Brett said, "I don't want these people anywhere near me."

Karyn turned, annoyed, and said, "These people are only trying to help you. And they have my permission to do whatever they want."

Brett's jaw dropped.

"Those in the most need of mental treatment are the last to admit it," Dr. Abscheulich said. "Brett, we are the professionals. You're in good hands here. We will schedule a thorough mental health examination for tomorrow morning and for now, I am prescribing you with Chlorpromazine at once." The doctor scribbled a note on a pad, handing the carbon copy to Karyn and the original to Nurse Rieck - who had suddenly appeared behind the doctor.

Brett briefly wondered how long she had been standing there and why he hadn't noticed her walk up.

In response to the prescription, Brett considered arguing. But he was aware that he was surrounded by individuals who had threatened him and didn't agree with him. To be safe, he nodded, but inside thought, "I am getting out of here." He attempted to look amicable.

Karyn thanked the doctor and he left the room. Karyn walked over to a nearby drinking fountain. It appeared she was downing more pills.

Nurse Rieck grabbed Brett's shoulder. Her hand felt like bones and ice. "Come with me, it's time for your afternoon dose."

She turned and walked over to the pill dispensary. She loaded four large capsules into a cup and handed it to Brett. Brett looked at them. They were a pinkish-orange color. "There's no way I'm swallowing these," he thought as he strolled toward the drinking fountain. Nurse Rieck glided by his side. He put the pills under his tongue, took a sip and pretended to gulp them down.

"Alright, open wide," Nurse Rieck said, and before Brett could even react she stuck a gloved finger into his mouth! She scooped out the four tablets onto the floor and scowled at Brett.

Karyn, who was a few feet away at this point, screamed at Brett, "I swear to god, you piece of -"

"There now, Brett," Nurse Rieck interrupted, "let's try this again."

She walked over to the pill bottle and poured out four more into a cup and brought them over to Brett.

With his mother and Nurse Rieck watching him, he felt he had no choice. He leaned down and took in water. He swallowed all four pills!

Chapter 12

Mitchell awoke with a start. It was 8:00 a.m.

He looked at his phone and there was a lot of communication from people wanting to help find the children or show their support somehow. "Hmmm . . . no update on Karyn, Brett or Elda," he thought. He was very worried. He threw on some clothes, deciding that boots and outdoors wear would be best.

Skipping breakfast, he left his large house and jumped in his car. He drove toward Karyn's house, a short distance from his own. On his way there, he hit a drive-through coffee cart for some caffeine and breakfast. He got a couple extra coffees.

He pulled up to Karyn's house and no one was there. He decided to call his longtime friend, Frank.

Mitchell and Frank had met in high school. Frank was a linebacker on the football team, while Mitchell was more academic and concentrated on shop class. It wasn't a typical friendship – jock and scholar. Mitchell had helped Frank with homework and tests.

Mitchell transferred over to Frank's high school junior year. Frank had attended since freshman year and the two of them were the same age. They met one day when a couple guys from the football team were harassing Mitchell. Frank stood up for Mitchell and got the guys to back off. They shared an interest in girls and had a similar sense of humor. Through the years, they had been through a lot as friends.

"Hello?" Frank said, answering his phone.

"Hey bud, it's Mitchell."

"What's happening, Mitch? Any news on the kids?" Frank responded.

"Not really," Mitchell said. "Like I told you, it looks like Karyn took the children."

Frank responded, "Any clues to where they're at?"

"No, I need help locating them."

"Of course, of course. I'll head over right now. Are you at Karyn's?"

"Yeah, I have a coffee waiting."

"Perfect. Man, I'm so sorry."

"It's okay. And Frank, we're going to search the forest, so dress appropriately."

They ended the call and Mitchell dialed Ernest. The detective told him they would be arriving shortly with the search dogs. They had checked at every hotel in a fifty-mile radius, to no avail. There was also nothing with the cab companies or bus system. They were looking into recent vehicle thefts and had calls into the only local car rental agency. The detective had also verified who the blood belonged to. It was Karyn's and it was evident, by blood found on the edge of the window opening, that Karyn had simply gotten cut while escaping. The detective was able to rush-order forensic testing to verify whose blood it was and Karyn's DNA was already on file from past occurrences. Mitchell thanked him and hung up.

The scene was clear in the daylight. Mitchell viewed the open basement window and looked across the backyard again.

If Karyn were a saner woman, Mitchell would not be worried. But she was prone to rash illogic. She lashed back at others and life. Her behavior was selfish and unpredictable.

Mitchell thought upon a memory from his relationship with Karyn. On one occasion, when Brett was but two years old, Mitchell and Karyn had had a spat. Karyn had accused Mitchell of being a bad father. Mitchell laughed in response and said, "Talk about the pot calling the kettle black!" Karyn had a fit. The fight occurred right before Mitchell left for work. When he returned home later that evening, he found Brett crying upstairs alone. Brett appeared to be hungry and Karyn was nowhere to be found. It was her responsibility to care for Brett during the day while Mitchell worked. Finding Brett by himself and neglected was quite a shock for Mitchell. Karyn didn't return for two days . . .

"Mitchell!" A yell from the detective pulled his attention from the memory. Mitchell jogged over to Ernest, who stood near a few officers. There were two leashed dogs.

"We are starting our search." Ernest pointed to two officers, "You, go to all houses on this route and check for Karyn and the children." He handed them a map with a sketched-out route to follow. Then he turned to two other officers and said, "You, take this route," – giving them a map of their own. "Officer Branson, you're with me and the search dogs."

"Mind if I tag along?" asked Mitchell.

"Wouldn't expect anything less," acknowledged Detective Ernest.

They headed into the house and down to the basement. Officer Branson held clothes to the dogs' noses. They sniffed to isolate the scent.

Suddenly, Mitchell heard loud knocking upstairs from the front door.

Chapter 13

Brett rushed to the nearest bathroom. He dropped to his knees in front of a toilet and shoved his fingers into the back of his throat. It caused a reflex. He kept at it. It was partially successful: he saw two of the capsules in the bowl beneath him.

Brett persisted in his attempted regurgitation until all four of the toxic caps rested in the water below. He then collapsed next to the toilet, his throat burning.

"I need to escape with Elda," Brett reminded himself.

He stood up and rinsed his mouth in the sink. Gulping water helped.

Meanwhile, Karyn was walking outside within the enclosed yard. With her were a couple of her fellow nurses. She had left Elda inside.

Elda was walking about asking for Brett and her mother. She was scared and had tears on her cheeks. She reached a hallway and walked through it. She tried turning the knobs. First door, locked. Second door, locked. Third door . . . Opened.

Elda looked in the room apprehensively. Inside were padded walls. The floor was cracked tile. Elda backed into the hallway and hid behind the doorway. She was terrified.

She took another look inside and saw a bed. It looked like someone was lying down.

Elda gasped. The person rose up and looked at her. It was a patient! Elda screamed.

Their hair was scraggly, thin and grey. Their face was wrinkled and pale. Elda watched in horror as the creature opened its dry, cracked lips and exposed rotten, dark teeth. Then they let out a shriek. Elda was frozen. The patient pointed at Elda and growled, causing Elda to scream again.

Nearby Brett heard a scream. It was his sister's voice. He ran to the bathroom door and threw it open. Looking left and right, he tried to locate where the noise had originated from. He guessed and headed right, into a large recreational room. There were about five patients lingering there. One of them was the familiar woman he had seen at breakfast. She was staring at him and it looked like she wanted to talk.

Brett had no time. He heard Elda's scream again: it was behind him. He had run the wrong direction; he should have taken a left outside the bathroom.

Brett headed back past the bathroom and turned into a hallway. He saw an open door and ran to it.

A woman was holding Elda in the air. Her hands were under Elda's armpits. She was carrying Elda toward the window. Without a word, Brett went over and in one motion he did a leg sweep and caught Elda. The woman fell hard on the floor and let out a shriek! Prior to being at Leiden Asylum, Brett had never had to utilize judo outside of class.

Brett held on to Elda and ran out of the room. Several feet away Nurse Rieck stood pointing at Brett, two large orderlies at her side.

"Wait," Brett pleaded, "this woman attacked Elda." Elda was clinging to Brett and shaking.

Brett looked back in the room and the woman was lying motionless on the bed. Funny, he hadn't heard her get off the floor.

Nurse Rieck replied, "Don't be silly, you brat. That woman is catatonic and hasn't moved on her own in years."

"Sorry, you're mistaken," Brett said. "My sister's life was put in danger by one of your patients. And I'm getting her out of here."

Nurse Rieck moved in closer. "Oh you silly boy, you're not going anywhere. Don't you realize? *You* are a patient."

Chapter 14

Clara had been a patient at Leiden Asylum for as long as she could remember. Her only bright memories of this life were from before being institutionalized. The only thing that mattered to her had been taken away long ago – her child.

Clara never knew her father and her mother was a maid. Clara was a beautiful, shy girl. If she were more outgoing, she could've been a movie star.

She was nineteen when she met the father of her child – Rodger. She was helping her mother clean a house and it happened to belong to his parents.

Clara had misjudged Rodger, thinking there was a future between them. Her naivety resulted in pregnancy. Rodger's interests lay solely in the act that results in children – not in having any.

Rodger's mother, Genna, disapproved of him having a relationship with anyone from the lower class. She discovered the clandestine, forthcoming baby and was utterly disgusted. She would take no part in a bastard grandchild and knew that Rodger had no intention of marrying Clara.

To Rodger's family, Clara was a nuisance to be disposed of.

On false charges, when she was three months pregnant, police burst into Clara's home and carted her off to Leiden Asylum. The accusation was that she had attempted to murder Genna. A weapon was found in Clara's house – one that Clara had never seen. A forged suicide note was included that "confessed" everything; it was written in her name.

Of course the evidence was invented by Genna and Rodger, but it didn't matter to the police. They had their orders. The final nail in the coffin was a written mental evaluation from a psychiatrist that Clara had never met. A Dr. Abscheulich. It labeled Clara mentally ill and ordered immediate involuntary commitment.

Due to the family's power and position, no trial was held. Clara was forcibly detained in the asylum.

She was made to deliver the baby in the institution, as opposed to a medical hospital. She held him for a few precious minutes and named him George. He had the most beautiful eyes. Her son was taken from her after birth and, presumably, had been put up for adoption.

She missed him every single day. The agony of her child being stolen away outweighed all other painful experiences in her life.

Clara numbed her pain with drugs. There was an unending supply at the asylum. Her days blurred together, one to the next. Eat, medicine, sleep . . .

She had tried to get away many times, each instance ending in pain and restraints – she was caught every time. Actually, in her years at the institution, no one had successfully fled. Dr. Abscheulich strategically placed staff throughout the asylum to keep everyone in. He always seemed to know where she was. After years at Leiden Asylum, Clara was left with the feeling that the doctor somehow sees everything.

Clara felt her life was like a motionless leaf, surrounded by dull clouds and resting in a still, murky pond.

But there was a moment recently that snapped Clara out of her haze. A family had entered the institution. She first saw them at breakfast.

Clara stood nearby and watched the family in the cafeteria. The woman appeared to be in her 30s. She had blue eyes, blonde hair, was of average height and was pretty. Despite her apparent beauty, she looked somewhat haggard and had bags under her eyes.

There was a little girl present as well. She had dirty blonde hair and green eyes. And lastly, a teenager with black hair and blue eyes. He was almost six feet tall and had an athletic build. They all looked familiar.

Her eyes locked on the boy. She felt as though she knew him and *must* speak with him.

Suddenly the mother slammed her hand on a table and berated the boy.

Clara looked away. She felt tired and headed to her room for a nap.

After her rest, Clara awoke and sat up in her bed. Her head was foggy. She decided to leave her room so she headed to the recreation area. She stood and stared at a wall, trying to recall what she had been doing . . .

Suddenly the teenage boy with black hair ran in. He looked at her. "Oh yes, the family," Clara recalled. Then, in the distance, there was a scream. The boy turned around and ran back out of the room.

Clara's breath stopped. Vague recollections stirred in her mind. Clouded remembrances were flowing in and out of her awareness. Why did she suddenly feel alive for the first time in over a decade? Why was she drawn to this family?

Why are these individuals the first new people that Clara has seen enter the institution in nearly two years?

Chapter 15

Mitchell ran up from the basement to see who the visitor at the front door was. He briefly hoped it could be someone that had information on his children, or even better, the children themselves. He snapped back to reality when he remembered the kids would never knock – they would simply enter the home.

He opened the door and it was Frank. "Of course," Mitchell thought, "I asked Frank to help."

"Hey man," Frank said. "Any update?"

"No," Mitchell said. "The police are here with search dogs and are going to track the kids. We're joining them."

The detective arrived at the top of the stairs. "Who do we have here?" he asked.

Frank walked over to the detective. "Frank, sir. Pleased to meet you," he said, shaking Ernest's hand.

"He's a long-time friend of the family and I invited him to join us on our search," Mitchell explained.

"Nice to meet you as well," the detective said to Frank. "My name is Ernest. Glad to have the help."

"The dogs are ready to head out," said Detective Ernest. "Let's do this."

The search party (composed of Ernest, Frank, Officer Branson, two locating dogs and Mitchell) started out in the backyard. Progress was slow. They began near the window and walked in a fairly straight path to the back fence.

They passed the fence and reached the sidewalk. There was a staticky sound from the detective's waist. It was the radio.

"Officer Myron, reporting in," it barked. "We've visited approximately twenty houses. No one has seen Ms. Slinger or the children."

"Alright," acknowledged Ernest, "thanks for the update."

The dogs continued their search. They sniffed left and right on the sidewalk.

They reached the middle of the street and stopped. Both dogs looked confused and sat down, as though they had lost the scent.

Mitchell crossed the street and stood in front of the forest. "Detective," he called back, "maybe they can pick up the trail over here."

The detective looked doubtful but abided.

They brought the dogs over. Their ears perked up and they started sniffing again. The dogs slowly made their way into the trees.

Mitchell's intuition had been correct, and they headed into the forest . . .

Chapter 16

Brett glared at Nurse Rieck.

"I am *not* a patient here," Brett argued.

"Have it your way," she responded. "Orderlies, restrain the boy."

The two brutes aggressively lumbered toward Brett. He set Elda down and stood his ground.

One of the men reached out to Brett. Brett used the force in the man's arm to toss him headfirst into a wall. There was a small amount of blood and the man fell onto his back with a dark welt on his forehead. The remaining orderly grinned and dove toward Brett.

Brett dodged and the man knocked Elda over. Elda wailed on the ground. Nurse Rieck was slowly approaching and the orderly was swinging at Brett.

Something inside Brett snapped. He wouldn't tolerate anyone harming his sister. In his martial arts training, he had learned certain moves that could be deadly. One move, Kani Basami, was banned but Brett mastered it outside of judo class. It consisted of wrapping your legs around your opponent's middle and slamming them on their spine. It can cause the back of your opponent's head to snap back onto the floor. When done on an untrained enemy with enough momentum and force, it can kill them – the back of their head caves in.

Without a second thought, Brett moved to the side, got his body in position and wrapped his legs around the orderly's midsection. Brett used the orderly's movement against him and flipped him backwards. The big man's head brutally slammed into the floor. There was a wet thud. Brett stood up and looked down. It was a hideous sight. Fragments, chunks and liquid. The man lay on his back, most likely deceased.

Nurse Rieck now stood just a few feet away. Brett turned his attention to Elda. She appeared to have a bruised knee and she was crying. The nurse held an injector needle and contemplated whether or not to attack.

Brett left her little time to think. He didn't want to attack the nurse so he picked up Elda and ran the opposite direction – his mind was racing. He had just attacked two orderlies and one or both of them were dead. His and his sister's lives were in danger. They had to escape.

He turned down four different hallways. The first hallway was empty, with every door in it shut. The second hallway was a different story. As Brett rushed through he glanced in a room. What he saw temporarily stopped his sprint. Brett stood outside the door. A man was stretched out across a table with small hooks stabbed through his skin at regular intervals. His wrists and ankles were bound in chains. There were marks on his skin - scabs and blood. The man's eyes flashed opened and bore into Brett. A coarse moan pushed out of the tortured male's throat. Brett broke away his gaze and continued his race through the halls, internally berating himself for stopping. The sight reinforced Brett's intent to exit.

The third hallway was another shut path - all doors shut. And then there! At the end of the fourth hall was Nurse Rieck. And she had brought reinforcements. There were four large men standing with her, apparently ready to follow whatever orders lay behind their general's lips. Brett decided against another attack. He whipped around and turned the corner he had just come from.

He could hear Nurse Rieck's voice yelling after him, "Come back here or we'll make you a permanent vegetable!"

Suddenly, a door in the hallway opened, a hand reached out and waved. Having very little time, Brett dashed into the room. He shut the door behind them and set Elda down.

It was a patient's cell, and inside was that strange, familiar woman . . .

Chapter 17

Karyn, who had been unemployed the majority of her life, was enjoying her new position. She was staying busy dispensing drugs to patients.

At the moment, she was preparing to serve Dr. Abscheulich in a surgery.

A nurse named Samanta was helping her get ready. "Karyn," Samanta said, "you need to wash your hands and put medical gloves on." Karyn obeyed and scrubbed at a sink.

Samanta further explained, "During the surgery you'll be expected to follow the doctor's orders precisely. You will need to hand him instruments, clean the patient, wipe up blood and perform other relatively simple actions. It is the doctor who has the hardest job, really."

"What if I mess up?" Karyn inquired.

"Oh don't worry about that. Dr. Abscheulich is very understanding. Just be professional and realize he has performed several thousand operations."

"But I don't have any formal medical training..."

"That's doesn't matter. You're just here as an assistant nurse. Stop worrying!"

Karyn nodded and snapped the surgical gloves on her hands as Dr. Abscheulich entered the room. "Shall we?" he asked.

Karyn and Samanta shadowed Dr. Abscheulich. They were led through a set of double doors and into a surgical hall. Inside the third room was a woman. She sat on the edge of a table.

The doctor approached her and asked, "How are we today, Ms. Jessica?"

The woman looked agitated. "Please . . . let me return to my room," Jessica pleaded. "I just want to be left to myself."

"Oh my dear Jessica, I am but going to *help* you. I have been informed that you have voices in your head. It is time we cut them out."

"No! Please! I am fine. Please . . ."

"Denial," Dr. Abscheulich said and looked to Samanta.

"Grab her right arm and hold her down," Samanta ordered Karyn. They approached Jessica and gripped her wrists. Nurse Samanta injected Jessica in the arm.

After a few moments, Jessica's body went limp. But her eyes remained alert and frantically swiveled between the nurses and doctor.

"Very good," purred Dr. Abscheulich. "Now, strap her to the table so I can get to work."

Karyn grabbed straps and cinched them to Jessica's right wrist and right ankle, copying Samanta's actions on the left.

"Hand me a skull saw," ordered the doctor. Samanta passed it to him and then wiped the patient's forehead.

"I am going to perform an advanced transorbital leucotomy," started the doctor as he moved next to the patient. "Typically, one severs the connective tissue leading to the prefrontal cortex, using an ice pick. But I figured out an improved way to perform this surgery. My method includes an incision and removal of a small section of brain that lies in the prefrontal lobes. In a way, I combine a lobotomy and leucotomy, but I feel I have isolated a more exact portion of the brain than other psychiatrists. A section of the prefrontal lobes that contains awareness. If you blot out a patient's awareness, they are no longer a menace to themselves or others.

"First off, we cut into the patient's skull." With that he started up the skull saw. He then drove the saw into Jessica's head. Karyn looked away. Blood spattered.

Karyn was nauseated by the sight. She retched. The doctor ceased cutting and glared at her. The patient kicked and jolted on the table as blood continued dripping on the floor. "Nurse Samanta, please escort Karyn out of the room and bring in a replacement nurse."

Karyn tried to resist the urge to throw up but failed. While most of the vomit landed in a trash receptacle, some missed. "Come now, Karyn," urged Samanta, "you must leave this room." Karyn was ushered to the hallway. Another nurse walked into the room, joining Dr. Abscheulich and Nurse Samanta.

The door was shut and locked in Karyn's face. She wiped her mouth on her sleeve. "I need a pill," she thought.

She stumbled down the hall to the capsule line. She grabbed herself two doses and made her way to the nearby drinking fountain. The nurse at the line looked at Karyn inquisitively and Karyn waved her away in response. She guzzled down the drugs and felt herself become desensitized.

"Are you okay, ma'am?" the nurse questioned.

"I'm fine now," Karyn answered. "But I am disappointed in myself. I let Dr. Abscheulich down. I am heading to my room for a doze."

Without any thought about her children, Karyn walked toward her room and said herself, "Dr. Abscheulich is an incredible doctor. I won't fail him again."

Chapter 18

Brett talked to the woman. "What is your name?"

"Clara," she responded. "Who are you?"

"I'm Brett and this is Elda," indicating the five-year-old clinging to his arm.

"It's nice to meet you both, but you must hide now! People are coming to find you and I'm afraid it won't be pleasant." Clara motioned for them to get under her bed. The bed was raised fairly high from the floor and a blanket draped over that would shield their presence.

Brett climbed underneath the bed and beckoned Elda to follow. They both lay on the cold stone floor covered in dust. Brett held his index finger to his lips to silence Elda. Behind his feet Brett noticed a large grate cover.

There was a pounding at the door. Clara opened it. It was Nurse Rieck. "Have you seen a boy and girl?" she asked.

"Several in this life," Clara responded.

"Don't be smart with me or you'll find yourself in the flashing room. Now, have you seen the recently admitted teenage boy and little girl?"

"No, Nurse Rieck. I have been in here alone for hours."

Nurse Rieck hesitated on whether or not to enter the room but due to worry that Brett may be running further away, she decided against it and headed back out to the hallway to continue her search.

Clara shut the door. "You can come out," she said.

Brett and Elda crawled out from the cobwebs and dusted themselves off. Elda sneezed.

"What is the 'flashing room'?" Brett asked.

Clara explained, "It is one of many torturous contraptions in this hell. The flashing room is a space where patients are sent for treatment. The person is strapped to a chair, electrodes are stuck to them and they are spun. As they spin, jolts of electricity enter their body while pictures flash on the walls around them. It is supposed to address psychosis. Dr. Abscheulich insists these therapies fix ailments. But in my opinion, it only makes things worse."

"What the hell? We need to leave this place . . ." He looked at Clara. "Why do you look so familiar?"

"I don't know but you guys do too. It's as if I've seen your family before. I feel like you've all awoken me from a deep sleep. I would like nothing more than to help you make your escape."

"How can you say that? You don't even know us. And obviously your own attempts at leaving failed – you're still here!"

Clara looked to the ground. Brett apologized. "I am just so shaken up by what I've seen and experienced here," he explained. "I appreciate your willingness to assist and I'll take any help I can get."

Brett made his way to the only window in the room. He looked out. It was getting dark now and he looked across the yard. There were paths running through the grass. He noticed a couple benches. There was fog along the ground and, again, there was that figure! A misty shadow. A familiar face . . . It raised a hand and pointed right at him!

The room door burst open behind him. Brett spun around, shocked, and saw Nurse Rieck enter with four orderlies. Brett positioned himself, ready to fight. But five against one weren't good odds. To top it off, Nurse Rieck had a small gun in her hand. On closer inspection, Brett saw that it was loaded with a tranquilizer dart.

Elda was frightened and ran behind her brother. The last thing Brett remembered was Nurse Rieck's finger pulling the trigger.

Chapter 19

Mitchell followed the dogs into the forest. It was cold out. A night had passed since his children went missing. The dogs were slow in their pursuit, smelling the ground and bottoms of plants.

The police, Frank and Mitchell were mostly silent. They were all looking back and forth across the forest for any clues as to the family's whereabouts.

Mitchell thought about Brett and how much he regretted having him spend so much time with Karyn. Their previous custody agreement granted Karyn majority custody. Mitchell had always tried to be a good father. He made time for his children when he had them, which was once a week. He was proud of both of them.

His thoughts then drifted to Karyn. How she had convinced him that she had changed ten years ago. He felt that she lured him back into a relationship by telling him how she had been all wrong and persuading him that she was different now.

Mitchell had eventually found that indeed she was different: she had become worse. Not only taking illicit drugs but continuing to sleep with other men. He found out too late, though; she hid it well. And before her misdeeds were uncovered, she was pregnant with yet another one of his children. He had doubted it but paternity tests had proven that he fathered both Elda and Brett.

Factually Mitchell worried about Elda more than Brett. Brett had martial arts and age on his side. Elda was virtually helpless. If they had run into the forest, how had she been eating? At this point over twelve hours must have passed since she last ate food. There is no lodging in the woods and it's doubtful they're living off the land.

Frank watched Mitchell. It looked as though he were deep in thought. "Hey, Mitch," Frank interjected, "the dogs are getting ahead."

Mitchell started walking toward the group. He caught up to them and asked Frank, "Have you seen anything promising?"

"No," Frank replied.

They walked side by side looking around the forest floor.

The detective looked over at Mitchell. "I can't imagine what he's going through," Ernest thought. "My children missing would be the worst possible feeling. At least we know the person that took them." Still, Detective Ernest could think of several cases of missing children that were never found, or worse.

One of the dogs barked. "I think he found something!" said Officer Branson. The detective, Frank and

Mitchell ran over. The dog had its nose to the ground and was walking as he sniffed.

The dog reached a torn black plastic garbage bag with clothes. It matched the one back at the house! Mitchell grabbed a handful of clothing. It was Elda's clothes!

"We're heading the right way!" Frank said.

Detective Ernest looked through the bag and around it. "There's no blood," he commented. "That's a good thing."

The good news was that they found more evidence. The bad news was they were far into the woods and the deeper they headed in the more danger the children were in.

The detective's cell phone rang. He answered and listened. "My god," he said, "that's terrible . . . I can't believe . . . But sir . . . I know, but . . . Yes, sir." He hung up.

"What?" Mitchell asked.

Ernest looked at him and said, "There's been a homicide."

Chapter 20

Elda was pounding on the door of the room. She had just awoken and it was early morning now. "Bro bro!" she cried.

Karyn rolled in her bed. "Shut up!" she yelled.

"Mama, where Brett?"

"Go to sleep, Elda. Be quiet!"

For fear of a spanking, Elda quieted down. She whimpered by the door and sat down. She missed her brother.

A scary woman had taken Brett away and Elda had been forced back into her room with Karyn. Elda was scared that Brett had been hurt. She had tried to get out last night but was subdued by her mother. She fell asleep late and woke up early.

Elda saw that her mom was asleep again and snoring. She tried the door; it was locked. She walked around the room trying to find another way out.

Elda just wanted to go home. She wanted to see her dad. She was too young to understand everything that was going on.

Elda loved her brother. She wanted to be like him. He paid attention to her. She of course loved Karyn and Mitchell as well but Brett was the only person in her life who was always around. Whereas her parents, due to divorce and other factors, were sporadic.

She stared out the window. It was a foggy morning. The door behind her clicked. Elda looked and gasped. It was a man. He had a cut-up face with stitches. He was massive, well over six feet tall. Elda tried to scream but he had already reached her. His hand covered her mouth and most of her head.

He picked her up and carried her out of the room. Elda attempted to struggle but it was pointless.

The man was wearing patients' clothes. He was heavy and strong. Should he choose to do so, he could end Elda with a squeeze.

Elda had never been more terrified in her entire life.

The hulking man shut the door and locked it while Karyn snored on.

Chapter 21

Brett awoke in a haze inside a black room. He could feel he was strapped to a table, bound at the waist, wrists and ankles. He struggled and attempted to wiggle free but he was cinched tight. The edges of his mouth were dry and raw. Someone had inserted a bit to his mouth. He couldn't talk and he was deathly thirsty.

His first thought was about Elda. He had to get free to ensure she was safe.

The lights, old hanging bulbs swinging from the ceiling, flashed on. Dr. Abscheulich entered the room. Brett blinked.

"Well, boy," the doctor said, "seems you've been up to no good. Mental disorders abound, but don't fret; I can fix you."

Brett continued to try to move around but was utterly restrained by his captors.

The doctor approached Brett. Brett noticed Nurse Rieck standing several feet behind. "This treatment is another invention of mine," the doctor began. "Step one: we open your eyes."

With that, Dr. Abscheulich reached down and forced open Brett's right eye. Brett tried to shout in protest but was rendered indiscernible by the bit. The doctor inserted something between Brett's eyelid and eyeball. It didn't cut Brett but it did coerce his eye open. He did the same thing to Brett's other eye.

Brett's eyes were stuck in an open position. It was extremely painful. There was a contraption above Brett's eyeballs that dispensed eye drops at regular intervals.

"Step two," Dr. Abscheulich said, "we medicate you." And with that the doctor injected Brett's arm. Brett immediately became dizzy.

Brett stiffened up. He prayed this hades would end. Brett looked on in horror as the doctor used a permanent marker to put a dot near his elbow and near his neck.

"Do you know what a pressure point is?" the doctor asked, expecting no answer. The doctor picked up a large needle. "There are certain nerve areas that are hyper-sensitive. When touched, they cause the utmost pain."

Dr. Abscheulich gripped Brett's right forearm and positioned the needle around Brett's elbow. He began inserting it into Brett's arm. The doctor stared directly into Brett's eyes as he tried to scream. Flames of agony shot through his body. His arms and spine pulsated.

"I hope you remember this the next time you consider disobeying me," the doctor said.

Brett saw dots in his eyes. The piece that had been jammed under his right eyelid became loose and fell out. His left eye was still forced open. The eye drops continued dripping from above. Brett forced his eyes to blink. The combination of the effort and liquid broke his left eye free as well.

The doctor was saying something. Brett was overwhelmed with pain and dope. He passed out.

Seconds later Brett was awoken with a splash of ice water. He moaned and blinked. His entire body ached. The doctor had removed the oversized needle from Brett's arm. There was a burning sensation and his arm was numb. Dr. Abscheulich stood nearby with a bucket and a sly smile.

"Now we are getting somewhere. During your seconds of unconsciousness, I instilled commands into your subliminal mind. The nerve I invaded with steel was your radial nerve. And now, we shall poke your suprascapular nerves and bury further dictates. I should have you know, the assaults on your nerves will only cause a temporary discomfort."

Brett didn't know what to do. He was trapped. He had never felt such pain. He had to hold on, if for nothing else than for Elda.

Then an explosion directly below his neck! The doctor had reinserted the needle, this time in a new location. Tears streamed down Brett's face and he struggled. Flame-hot suffering pervaded his body. Once again, but this time for much longer, Brett's world went black.

Chapter 22

Clara watched in shock as Brett was tranquilized. An orderly shoved her on the bed and dragged Brett across the floor and out of the room. Another orderly approached Elda, picked her up and carried her out of the room.

Clara snapped out of her daze and walked after the children but her collar was roughly grasped by a large orderly. She felt a sting in her neck – she was being sedated. She tried to wrestle free but she drifted away.

Clara didn't know how much time passed, but when she regained consciousness her room was empty. It took a few minutes for the haziness to pass. It all came back to her . . . The boy and girl had been taken. She didn't know where they were taken but she was determined to locate them.

Clara stood up and stepped toward the door. She tried the handle and it was locked. She glanced out the small barred window in her door just as a massive figure lumbered past. It was Masheck! She suddenly couldn't breathe.

Masheck was a patient that Dr. Abscheulich used as a test subject in many operations. Masheck was a huge man, well over 6 feet tall and around three hundred pounds in bulk. Clara heard he was ex-military. The doctor was known to rid the institution of difficult cases by throwing them in a cell with Masheck. It was a constant threat hanging over the head of patients. Yes, Masheck had murdered multiple employees and patients. One of the countless reasons Clara wished to flee this place.

Clara noticed he was carrying something . . . It was the girl, Elda! Clara frantically shook the door handle.

Masheck continued on out of sight and didn't notice Clara. Clara was panic-stricken. She stared into the hall, wanting Masheck to return with the girl.

Clara recalled an incident wherein one of her fellow patients, Lester, had punched one of the staff. As punishment, he was made to spend the night in Masheck's cell. Clara never saw Lester again.

She walked over to a nearby wall panel and pulled it back. Behind it was a crude map that she had kept. As time went by, she had learned that escaping the institution proved virtually impossible. Orderlies and other institution staff were carefully placed throughout the premises. After many attempts she discovered one potential path - the ventilation system. After several failed shots, she finally made it to a vent that led outside the building. But even then she didn't open the vent due to disturbing nearby employees and she hadn't figured out how to get past the locked gate outside. There was no way to quietly open the final vent cover. But she was committed to utilizing this map in freeing the children because it was the best chance they had at escape. She would simply have to work with Brett on solving the final vent and outside gate.

Then there was a click at the door and it opened. A nurse stood in the doorway and said, "It's pill time. Come to the main hall." Clara breathed a sigh of relief and complied – she was happy to be freed from her room because it meant she could now search for the children.

Clara was served a cupful of capsules from Karyn. Clara introduced herself and Karyn forced a smile. "Are you aware of the present location of your children?" Clara asked.

Karyn's demeanor instantly warped. "Shut up, patient!" she hissed, "The less they are underfoot and out of my hair, the better. Get out of my face!"

Clara went to the nearest bathroom and flushed the tablets down the toilet. She exited and made her way to a nearby hallway to start the search. She attempted looking as inconspicuous as possible. Luckily, at this time of day patients typically wandered about.

Being aware of the general layout of the institution, Clara first headed to Masheck's room at the quickest pace possible that wouldn't attract attention.

During the short trek, nothing eventful occurred, but Clara did notice that there seemed to be more nurses and orderlies about than normal, with an excessive amount of eying.

She arrived at Masheck's room and found it barren. "Well," she thought, "I'd better hurry up and find these guys." It was the first time in many years that Clara felt a purpose about anything. She decided to start in the confinement hall – a section of the institution wherein rooms were located for involuntarily storing patients.

Clara rushed around a few turns and came to the start of the confinement area. It was a hallway lined with locked cells of various assortments.

She glanced in the first door. It was pitch black. She moved to the second door and looked through the window. There was a man chained and hanging from the ceiling. His wrists were bound and pulled tight. His ankles were strapped and pulled - he was elevated about a foot from the floor. There was blood and gashes on his body. All of a sudden the man jolted and looked up. To Clara's surprise he started laughing. Black liquid expelled from his mouth and dripped down his injured body. Clara tore her eyes away, shuddered and walked to the next door.

Inside it was a man staring at a projector screen. He was sitting on a spiked chair which appeared to be stabbing his lower body. He was being forced to watch some sort of film as he sat in torture. Clara quickly moved on to the following doorway.

This door was open. The room was dark. Clara entered to search for Elda and Brett. There was a scurry in the back corner. "Hello?" she ventured. A shadow jumped out at her and grabbed her throat. Clara fell into the wall behind her. Atop her was a bony woman with a torn hospital gown. The woman's features were defaced. Clara pushed back – the woman seemed to be trying to bite at Clara.

Clara kicked hard with both feet and the woman was flung off her and slid into the darkness. Clara used this opportunity to make her escape. She stood up and ran out the door. The ugly woman gave chase. Clara turned two hallways. As she passed rooms she scanned for Brett or Elda. She looked behind and the disfigured woman was closing in.

Clara turned another corner and as she sprinted down the hall, she looked through a door's window and saw Brett in a surgical room!

Chapter 23

Mitchell was frantic and looked wonderingly at the detective. "What happened? What do you mean there's been a murder? Who died?"

The detective immediately put Mitchell at ease. "I apologize. That was immensely inconsiderate of me. The call had nothing to do with your family. There was a homicide involving the mayor's son. Due to the fact that a VIP was present, the chief wants me all over it. Not to mention the fact that I'm a homicide detective and it's a homicide. And, thankfully, finding your kids isn't a homicide."

Frank entered in the conversation. "So, that means you're not going to help us anymore?"

Detective Ernest frowned. "No. But it does mean that I need to get started on this murder investigation as my priority."

"So, wait," Mitchell said, "the mayor's son is dead?"

"No, no," the detective answered. "The mayor's son was present at the time of the incident. Basically, it looks like someone intentionally ran over somebody and the mayor's son was nearby when it occurred. Not meaning that he killed someone, but due to his being around when the death occurred, it is vital that I handle this intelligently and sensitively. For PR reasons. Now if you'll excuse me, I have to get on this. Officer Branson, please stay here and continue the search. Don't worry everyone, I'll be back as soon as possible."

Mitchell shook Ernest's hand and the detective left.

The officer, Mitchell and Frank continued the search. After several minutes, it appeared the dogs were sort of wandering aimlessly. The dogs were circling and occasionally sat and sniffed the air. So they took them back to the bag of clothes to have them smell the items again.

The dogs then slowly crept through the forest. The men followed, desperately looking for any further clues. After another hour or so, it was painfully apparent that this search had hit a dead end. The dogs kept returning to the bag and looked confused. Officer Branson's cell phone rang. He stepped a few feet away to take the call.

Frank placed his hand on Mitchell's shoulder. "Hey brother, we will find them. I think we should organize an expanded search. Your children are fine. I'm in this with you."

The officer ended the call and joined Mitchell and Frank. He said, "Looks like I'm needed down at the station. I'm sorry but I have to go."

Mitchell responded, "Officer Branson, we need to keep looking. These are my kids we're talking about and the detective already left."

"I'm sorry sir, orders are orders. And as you know, your kids don't qualify as missing persons until they've been gone for 24 hours. I need to leave."

"This is ridiculous. My daughter is five. If they're in this forest that means they haven't eaten since maybe dinner time last night. It's just not safe. I need your help."

"The trail has gone cold. The dogs are at a loss. Listen, we can organize a larger search party tomorrow -"

"Tomorrow? Are you crazy? Another night of them lost? No way!"

"Calm down, sir. In a matter of hours they'll officially be missing persons. We can then utilize media and organize search parties. But like it or not, I have to go."

Mitchell turned away and resisted any further outburst. Frank acknowledged the officer and attempted to raise Mitchell's spirits. "We will find them."

Mitchell's mind raced with all that could be going wrong. It's common knowledge that when it comes to missing people, time is your greatest enemy.

As he looked out across the forest, Mitchell knew that each passing moment meant less likelihood of a positive outcome.

Chapter 24

Karyn had always felt the odds were against her. In her eyes, Mitchell had been a horrid partner. He always made her feel like he was better than she was. She didn't like how he talked down to her or pitted the children against her.

They had been on and off for several years. It was always Mitchell's excessive work schedule that drove Karyn into the arms of other men. His holier-than-thou attitude and constant busyness were more than she could bear. Karyn felt Mitchell didn't give her the attention she deserved. She needed more time and interest than Mitchell gave her.

Not only that, but Brett far preferred Mitchell. Karyn knew it must be that Mitchell spoke poorly of her when she wasn't around. He must be stuffing her son's head with lies.

"It's all Mitchell's fault," Karyn told herself. "A terrible man I should have avoided altogether. I hate him."

Karyn decided to walk outside the institution for a minute because she had a little bit of time to kill before manning her post. She stepped over to the front door of the asylum. There were four large orderlies standing around it – appearing to be guarding the door. "Can I go out for a stroll?" Karyn asked one of them. He glared and grunted. They let her out.

She walked down the steps. It was chilly outside and there was a lot of fog. Several feet ahead of her was the imposing gate. She looked around. There were small paths through the grass leading around the grounds. The guards were staring at her from the front door.

Karyn chose a path and walked through the foggy grass. She noticed a couple benches and looked over at the fence. It was massive and the spikes at the top were menacing. She observed a couple staff trailing behind her. "Are they following me?" she thought.

She continued her walk and saw an old woman sitting still on a bench. Karyn looked at her as she walked past. The woman was staring solidly at the ground, unblinking.

Karyn decided to circle back toward the asylum. She noticed some stone objects over to her left. She wandered over and saw they were tombstones. The graves were cracked and appeared to have been assaulted by years of weather. A small sign lay nearby that read "Staff Graveyard." She shuddered. "Creepy . . ." she thought. She leaned in to read some of the names but heard, "Karyn!"

She whipped around to see Samanta standing by the front door of the asylum. "We need you back here!" Samanta yelled over.

Karyn jogged over, entered the institution and walked over to the pill line, behind the counter. She began dispensing patients their dose of drugs. She was disappointed in herself for not behaving more professionally during the surgery.

"I think next time, you should take anti-nausea medicine beforehand," Samanta advised. "Don't beat yourself up, Karyn; Dr. Abscheulich is a progressive psychiatrist. Far beyond all others in skill and precision. His methods may take some getting used to, but you'll get there."

Karyn nodded in response.

Karyn continued serving pills and a blonde female patient asked her about her children. This was annoying for Karyn, so she snapped in response. What right did this young woman have prodding into Karyn's business?

The final patient collected their cup and Karyn slumped back in a chair. Karyn grabbed some capsules for herself and gulped them down. Something to take the edge off.

Samanta looked over and said, "It looks like Dr. Abscheulich wants you to help with another surgery."

"So soon?" inquired Karyn.

"Yes, he sees a lot of potential in you."

"I'd be glad to help."

"Good; meet us in Surgery Room C in ten minutes. Oh, and take these." Samanta handed Karyn a couple more pills.

Karyn was excited for a second chance! She walked to her room and used the sink to swallow the pills Samanta provided – she figured they must be anti-nausea medication.

"I wonder what the brats are up to?" she pondered briefly. "Hopefully they are staying out of trouble."

Karyn felt a little hazy and tired. She stiffened herself up and made her way to the surgical room.

As she passed by Room A, she looked in and saw a man inside lying face down on a table. An overweight doctor was operating on the man's knee. Karyn looked closer – the patient's leg was missing from the knee down. It appeared that the leg had been amputated above the shin. The doctor was stitching something onto the knee . . . Karyn gasped! He was sewing a human arm to the patient's knee!

Karyn gazed in horror as the patient pushed himself up, turned his head toward her and smiled! She fell backward away from the door and landed on her posterior.

Karyn sat for a moment, not daring to look back in, and then stood up and made her way to Room C – intentionally avoiding looking in Room B during her short trek. She had been thoroughly creeped out by the sight of a strange surgery and the patient's grinning face. "I am not a trained doctor," Karyn told herself, "so I am in no position to judge these people. The patients are disturbed and the doctors know what they're doing." She arrived at Room C.

The room was cold and dark. She turned on the light. It was the same room where she had helped on the first surgery. The floor had a couple damp spots and there were various instruments near a surgical table.

Samanta and Nurse Rieck entered the room. Karyn smiled at them both.

"Well, so who is the sick person we will operate on now?" Karyn asked.

"Oh my dear girl," Nurse Rieck replied. "It is to be your surgery. *You're* the subject today. It is time we excavate your rotted ailments!"

Chapter 25

The ugly woman tackled Clara from behind. Clara felt a sharp pain in her right forearm. The nasty lady was biting her! Clara hit at the woman's head. This time getting away wasn't as easy. They wrestled on the floor. Clara kicked and punched as the woman shrieked and bit.

Clara finally got loose, jumped up and started her run again. With the deranged woman on her heels, Clara turned right and at the end of the hallway were two hefty orderlies! She had to think fast.

"Please help!" Clara yelled. "This woman is attacking hospital staff!" She knew that the staff couldn't care less about patients but assaulting institution personnel was considered a serious offense.

The two men hulked toward Clara. The nasty woman stopped and glared. She then let out a hideous scream. The orderlies shoved her to the ground and Clara jetted. "Hey! Get back here!" one of the men bellowed. "You're both going to lockup!"

Clara ran for about a minute at top sprint and came to a row of lockers. She chose one at random. Locked! She could hear the sound of running footsteps. She tried another locker; it was unlocked. She climbed inside, barely fit, and shut the door.

One of the orderlies made his way down the hall. Clara held her breath, terrified she would be discovered. He jogged right past her and turned a corner. He was out of sight. Clara waited for about a minute and heard nothing.

She slowly exited the locker and tiptoed back to the room she had seen Brett in. He was alone and appeared to be unconscious. Clara turned the door handle and entered the room. She walked over and unstrapped his arms and legs.

Brett looked terrible. He had a couple of small scabs on his body and dark circles under his eyes and he was out cold. Clara shook him gently. "Brett?" she asked. No response. She shook him harder. Nothing.

Clara was worried that someone would arrive soon. She looked around the room for something to wake him with and, amongst various items, she saw a bucket and a sink. She picked the bucket up and filled it with water. Splash! Brett coughed.

"What . . . the . . ." he grumbled. He moved around and turned his head. He squinted at Clara and pleaded, "No more. Help me . . . Please."

Clara grabbed Brett's arm and pulled at him. "Come on, we need to go. We have to find your sister." That seemed to get Brett's attention.

"Elda . . ." he said. He stood up, shakily, and stumbled toward the door with Clara.

Brett was wincing from sharp pains. He was dizzy, nauseous, and his head ached. He looked at Clara. "Thank you." He paused and then asked, "Where's my sister?"

"I don't know," Clara responded. "We have to check the patient rooms. I've been through a couple areas. We can pick up where I left off."

They walked over to a nearby hallway and looked into rooms. They took separate sides of the hall. Brett was struggling but slowly regained his strength with each step. The necessity of locating Elda was a strong motivating force for him.

Unlike Clara's earlier search, they found something faster this time.

Clara looked in and saw Masheck! He was holding a doll in his left hand. His scarred face was twisted into a hideous smile.

In his right hand, he held Elda . . .

Chapter 26

Mitchell felt anger, fear and sadness, and was battling hopelessness. He wished he knew his children were out of harm's way.

He stood in the woods. Frank was nearby peering at the forest floor, vainly attempting to discern a trail that the dogs missed.

Mitchell recalled how volatile Karyn could be. Seemingly happy and content one moment, and pouring out a critical tirade the next. "Taking the kids was reckless enough," Mitchell thought. "Could she have hurt them as well?"

Brett had told him that Karyn sometimes hit him and Elda. It was one of the reasons Brett wanted to learn judo - self-defense. It also was a factor in Mitchell gaining custody of the children. While far from a perfect dad, Mitchell didn't believe in corporal discipline.

It had now been almost 24 hours since the children went missing. The combination of stress and lack of sleep got the best of Mitchell and he teared up. He sat roughly on a nearby stump.

He put his head in his hands. "It's been years of this," he thought. Karyn's persistently unpredictable, immature and downright evil behavior had worn on Mitchell and he'd had enough.

Frank looked over and decided to give Mitchell some space. He picked up his phone and posted a message online, inviting friends to meet them at the edge of the forest at 6:30 p.m. to help in the search.

After a few moments, Frank said, "Come on, man. Let's grab a bite and then hit the search again. Besides, I've got some help coming soon."

Mitchell stood up and walked over. They trod back toward the main road. "You remember that time that Karyn went off on me?" Frank asked.

"Which one?" Mitchell asked.

"It was that night where we had an office party downtown to celebrate our biggest year to date. We had a blast; karaoke, James got thrown out of the bar . . . I drove you home."

"Oh, yeah. Man, I'm sorry about that."

"It's not your fault. But anyways, we pulled up and Karyn was outside wearing only a t-shirt. She was holding a pan and she cracked my windshield!"

"Why are you saying this?"

"I don't know, man. It's just that Karyn's loopy and I get why you're worried. I am too. For what it's worth, I'm not going anywhere. We're finding these guys."

Mitchell smiled weakly and patted Frank on the back.

They reached the main road. "So," Frank began, "where do you want to eat?"

They walked a couple blocks and grabbed some cheeseburgers. It felt good to eat again. They swigged some coffee and prepared to hit the road again.

As they stepped back toward the forest, Mitchell saw a large crowd of people. He started making out faces. They were family, friends, associates . . . He turned to Frank. "Thank you."

"Don't thank me," Frank responded as he pointed at the group of helping hands.

There was even a news van there interviewing people.

Mitchell's phone rang. It was the detective.

Chapter 27

Brett yelled and kicked the door. Clara moved back to give him room. Masheck was laughing inside the room. He tossed Elda onto a nearby mattress. Her eyes were shut and she wasn't moving.

Brett kicked again and the hinges creaked. Masheck stood up and growled. Brett was shocked by Masheck's size. He looked like a professional wrestler that swallowed a football player. He lumbered over and reached for the door.

Brett walked backwards and took a stance. He scanned his environment – no weapons. Masheck tore the door from its hinges and threw it at Brett. Brett sidestepped but the door smashed into his shoulder. He was spun around and landed on the floor. Clara ran to the end of the hall, behind Brett.

Masheck snickered and stomped over to Brett. Brett somersaulted backward to his feet. Masheck extended his tree trunk of an arm right toward Brett's face. Brett tried to grasp his wrist and throw him but Masheck easily resisted.

Masheck's hand clamped on Brett's face and he squeezed. Brett screamed in pain. In seconds he felt that his face would cave in. Brett kicked and wriggled to get free.

Suddenly, a datum Brett had learned in martial arts came to mind. "There isn't a move for every possible situation. In real life, sometimes you have to improvise, surprise your enemy and play dirty."

Brett bit down on Masheck's hand as hard as he could and felt blood stream into his mouth. Masheck bellowed and released his grip. Brett quickly rolled back and felt his face: no permanent damage.

Brett rapidly analyzed the situation. There was no way he could move this man. He must concentrate on small, sensitive body parts: eyes, nose, ears, fingers . . . Masheck clenched his fists and roared. He jogged over and swung at Brett. Brett ducked and Masheck's fist made a hole in the wall the size of a bowling ball.

Brett head-butted Masheck's nose. More blood. Masheck stumbled back and licked at the blood coming down his face. He smiled.

Brett went on the offensive and toe kicked toward Masheck's face. Masheck saw it coming and grabbed Brett by the leg and swung him around like a rag doll. Brett tumbled and skidded several feet down the hallway. He could feel his body bruising and the air was knocked from his lungs.

Clara shrieked. It appeared that Masheck had turned his attention to her. Brett gasped for air and forced himself up. He could feel his muscles trembling. He hopped up and sped over to Masheck, who had his back turned. He jumped up on Masheck's back, braced his thumb, reached around and shoved it as hard as he could into the beast's eye.

Masheck howled and reached back to grab Brett but Brett hopped off. Brett looked down and saw blood on his thumb. Masheck turned around and reached for Brett. Brett decided to risk another attack and leapt backwards. He caught himself on his hands and lifted his right leg with all his might as though kicking a soccer ball. Brett's foot smashed in between Masheck's legs and Brett felt a squish.

Masheck fell to the floor, holding himself and immobilized. Clara looked to Brett and said, "Thank god."

Brett stared at the heaving monster of a man, and solemnly replied, "No. He stole my sister. No one is safe as long as he is wandering around here."

Brett stood over Masheck. One of Masheck's eyes was rendered useless, his nose was smashed and he would probably never have children. Brett only had moments to act. He sprinted into Masheck's room, noticed that Elda was waking up, and he grabbed a metal chair. He ran it back over to Masheck, who appeared to be trying to sit up.

Brett lifted the steel chair, aimed one of its legs carefully and . . . Smash! Clara looked away.

"Bro bro!" Elda yelled. She hopped over to him.

"Elda!" Brett said. "Are you hurt?"

"No owies. Scary man pretended I was a doll." Brett searched over Elda's body. There were a couple small bruises but no abrasions. He had her move some of her joints and she giggled.

"Thank god," Brett whispered.

Brett noticed a window in the room. It, though barred, showed the outdoors. Outside it was gloomy and foggy. Again, Brett observed that misty, human-like shape . . . It was like a ghost, with cloudy eyes boring into his soul. "It's a person," Brett thought. "Why can't I make out who it is? I know that person . . ."

"Ew!" Elda cried, "That man has chair in his head," referring to the steel leg stabbed into Masheck's left eye socket. He was dead.

Chapter 28

Karyn was shocked. She didn't realize that she had been called there for her own operation.

"But," she quavered, "I thought I was a nurse?"

"Come now," Nurse Rieck said. "All of the staff undergo surgeries here at Leiden Asylum. This is Dr. Abscheulich we're talking about. A prestigious genius. You should feel honored. People pay tens of thousands of dollars for his help and you're getting treatment for free."

Karyn was nervous. Should she try to leave? Should she go with it? Before she could make up her mind, Nurse Rieck grabbed her wrist. Karyn was injected. Two more nurses entered the room. The doctor was fiddling with a large machine close by.

The additional nurses approached Karyn and had evil grins on their faces. One of them had a scar below the hairline on her forehead.

Karyn felt woozy and fell onto the surgical table. She barely felt the hands binding her.

The room was spinning and blurred. She felt cold probes touching her temples. Dr. Abscheulich was standing over her saying something. She couldn't make it out.

Then a jolt! Karyn felt electricity enter her body. She could feel the sensation of burning nerve channels. She perceived small sections within herself dying.

The room went white and spots danced before her eyes. Again a jolt! Her body convulsed. She was utterly unable to control her movements. She wanted to leave but was trapped.

Karyn tried to cry and scream but the electric shock was causing her body to disobey.

The doctor was still talking. But Karyn wasn't able to hear anything he was saying.

Karyn thought she must be dying.

Memories of Mitchell flashed in her mind. They had been through so much together, ups and downs – mostly downs. Then for the first time since entering the asylum, she wanted to see Brett and Elda. "I have to get out of here with them," she thought as pain ripped into her. For a moment, she might have actually missed them.

Waves of electricity tore through her. She felt memories and thoughts slip away. White lights and crackling dominated her mind until it went blank. Years of life washed away by minutes of inhumane torture.

The overwhelming pain caused Karyn to lose consciousness.

Chapter 29

Mitchell answered his phone. "Hello?"

"Hi," Detective Ernest started. "Well, it looks like I can return for the search. That other case is under control now."

"Oh?"

"Yeah, the mayor's son is in the clear. Wrong place, wrong time."

"Well, that's great I guess. What happened?"

"I can't give any names but basically he was driving down a street and witnessed a drunk driver, in a separate car, run over a pedestrian. Anyways, open–and–shut case. The driver is in custody and the mayor's son is in the clear. None of that matters though; what matters is that the captain said I can go flat-out on this search now."

"Awesome. Are my kids missing persons yet?"

"Not exactly. Still two hours or so, but that doesn't matter. I'm coming back with three officers and the dogs. Plus, I just saw on the news that you've got some people there willing to help too."

"Yes, sir. The media found out somehow. Alright, see you soon, Detective. Thank you."

"Thanks, Mitchell. Wait for me and we can coordinate a search grid. See you shortly." They ended the call.

Frank said, "It looks like my online post got some attention. I may have also reached out to a couple local news stations before we met up this morning." Mitchell smiled at Frank and thanked him, feeling lucky to have such a great friend. They'd known each other for about twenty years.

Mitchell spent a few minutes greeting people in the crowd, anxious for the detective's arrival so the hunt could start again. He knew most of the individuals present and had to re-explain several times that Karyn had evidently taken the children in response to being told that Mitchell had been granted full custody.

A reporter jogged over to Mitchell, right as Detective Ernest pulled up in his car, holding a microphone. "Sir," she asked, "can we ask you some questions that may help in the search for your kids?"

Mitchell paused and then said, "Sure."

A light and camera were directed at the reporter and Mitchell.

"This is Rebecca Furley with Channel 6 News," the reporter said. "I have here Mitchell Slinger, father to two missing children. We join him in a large search party. Mr. Slinger, what do you think happened to your kids?"

"Well," Mitchell began, "I came by to pick them up from their mother's last night and they weren't there. They've been missing now for one full day and we found some of their clothing in the woods. I -"

"Is it true that their mother kidnapped them?

"I don't know if -"

"And isn't it true that she is an addict? With a history of violence?"

"Now listen here, I just want to find my children. I'm not interested in an interview about our personal life. We -"

"But Mr. Slinger, all of these facts *are* relevant to finding your kids. Are you denying their mother's involvement in their disappearance?" Mitchell's face flushed.

Detective Ernest had walked over and cut in. "Ma'am, we have little evidence to determine what happened beyond the fact that apparently Karyn and the children entered these woods. And every minute we spend here yapping is a minute lost on our search. Here's what to tell your viewers: if you have any information regarding the disappearance of Karyn Aargon Slinger, Brett Slinger or Elda Slinger, contact the authorities immediately. Otherwise, come on down here with a flashlight and a warm coat and help us out!" He then put his hand on the front of the camera and pushed down, signifying the end of the broadcast.

The reporter slumped, dumbfounded, and the detective and Mitchell walked off.

The detective sprawled a map across the side of the news van and Frank held up one of the corners. People gathered around.

"Alright, everyone!" Ernest stated loudly, "We are going to comb through the forest. Each person will spread out ten feet from the next and we will make our way in a straight line, heading west. If you find anything, please inform a police officer. Okay, let's head out!"

The police officers were handing out flashlights to anyone that needed it. It was nearly dusk.

Mitchell stood between the detective and Frank. They retraced their earlier path and reached the clothes again. They walked for several minutes. This time, the detective had a forensic team collect all the evidence and inspect everything in more detail.

The same two dogs were on the search and reacted similarly.

There were about fifty people spread across the woods.

It was starting to get dark. Mitchell noticed a fog beginning to form on the forest floor. It was a creepy setting.

The line of people made their way through the forest, scanning the ground, bushes, trees . . .

To his left, Frank saw a small creek. He walked over to it and bent down to inspect it. His cell phone fell out of his breast pocket, into the water. "Oh no!" Frank exclaimed. He picked it up and put it into his pocket.

Frank then observed a small trail to the left and decided to follow it. He hadn't noticed it on the previous search. Mitchell was looking into a large bush several feet away and the detective was shining his flashlight back and forth in a methodical pattern.

Frank quickened his pace. Yes, it appeared to be a very old trail – covered with leaves and brush. He jogged down the path for a couple minutes and realized he was alone. "Over here!" he yelled. Silence. It was getting quite dark now. Frank pulled out his cell phone and discovered the earlier bath had broken it completely. He yelled again. Nothing.

He debated within himself whether or not to continue down the covered trail or to turn back. An image of Brett and Elda flashed in his mind. He decided to continue with the trail.

He walked down the foggy, nearly invisible path. In the darkness and by himself.

Chapter 30

Brett stood over Masheck's body, pondering whether or not he should hide it or just run. The choice was made for him when he heard multiple footsteps approaching.

Brett held Elda's hand and took her around a corner. Clara whispered, "We can hide in my room. There's a ventilation shaft under my bed that's hidden from view." The pursuing footsteps stopped and they could hear voices talking, assumingly about the body.

Elda and Brett followed Clara through several empty hallways to her room. They shut the door behind them. Elda was tired and passed out on the bed.

"Listen," Brett said to Clara, "I really appreciate your help. You saved my life and helped me find my sister. But we need to get out of here. They caught us here last time. Elda and I need to escape and I want you to come with us."

Clara dug for her map and pulled it out. "Here," she said, showing it to Brett. "It took me years and I was nearly caught several times, but I found a way out through the ventilation system. It was installed years ago and is big enough for us to crawl through."

Brett looked at the map. It was a large piece of very old paper with a layout of the institution scrawled on it. In heavy black ink, the ventilation system was drawn out. He traced his finger over it and saw it lead to a shaft about twenty feet from the front door of the asylum.

"Why don't we just go out the front door when the guards are away or something?" Brett asked. "I'm sure there're lots of ways out of here."

"Haven't you seen?" Clara said. "There are always staff guarding all exits. No one's ever escaped in the decades I've been here."

Clara couldn't have been more than thirty years old. "How had she been there decades?" Brett thought to himself.

"Fine," Brett replied. "You've been right so far. How do we escape?"

"Well, it won't be that easy. First of all, crawling through the ventilation shafts is very loud and they take you through many rooms and offices. So, we have to time it right. And second of all, when you reach the outside vent, we will need to figure out how to get past the guards and through the locked gate."

"Okay, so what do we do?"

"We need to go during a meal time. And I don't know what to do about the outside guards or the gate."

"Alright. Well, I say we head out ASAP and I'll figure out the guards and fence when we get there. I need to get you girls to safety."

Brett and Clara jointly swiveled their heads toward the door. There was a noise; someone was coming. "I'll handle them," Clara hissed. "You and Elda need to hide in the vent." Clara shoved the map into his hands and pushed him back. Brett tried to argue but Clara walked to the door and put her hand on the handle.

Brett quickly grabbed Elda and whispered, "Remember the quiet game? We need to play it now." They went under the bed and Brett removed the vent cover. Clara had already taken the screws out. He climbed in and beckoned Elda to join him. They huddled in the dust-ridden shaft and overheard muffled voices. Brett placed the vent cover back in place the best he could and moments later he saw a couple pairs of feet through the cover.

He didn't see Clara. He observed several more people enter the room. "We need to leave now or they'll find us," Brett thought to himself. He began climbing through the ventilation system, Elda following.

"How much longer do I have to be quiet?" Elda asked. Brett shushed her and she looked scared.

"I'm sorry," Brett apologized. "Listen, Elda, there are bad guys trying to get us. I need you to be brave and to be quiet. I am going to get us out of here. Just follow me." Elda nodded in response.

Brett looked over the map. It appeared they had a ways to go. Luckily, light streamed in through the vent covers and they could see. They crawled along. The shafts creaked with each movement. Brett was amazed they hadn't been found out yet. He looked through each vent cover as they made their way past. The first two were empty rooms. Then a large file room. They kept going and Brett heard voices. He looked through the vent cover. It was a large group of staff, doing some sort of a meeting.

There was no way they would get past them without being heard. Brett held his finger to his lips to remind Elda to be silent and they carefully moved backwards.

Brett decided to wait in the shaft that ran through the file room until the meeting ended. Elda had made a little doll out of lint and was, thankfully, quietly keeping to herself.

Brett thought back to how Karyn would bring home strange men. When he was younger, he had thought they were friends or something. But at a certain age he realized what was really going on.

The thing that bugged him the most was when she brought men home around Elda. One time recently, Karyn stumbled in with a heavily tattooed man that looked to be only a couple years older than Brett. The man looked and sounded like an illiterate drug addict. Brett took Elda upstairs and played hide and seek with her – trying to keep her away from the negative environment.

"Even though that was bad, it's nowhere near as terrible as this place," Brett thought to himself as he looked through the vent cover to inspect the file room. There were rows of alphabetized filing cabinets. "Must be patient files," Brett mumbled as Elda continued her silent dust bunny game. He then noticed a desk with an open folder lying on top. Clear as day he could see the patient's name: Brett Slinger.

Chapter 31

Mitchell called out Frank's name. "Great," he thought, "now Frank's missing too."

"Don't worry about it," Detective Ernest said. "I'm sure he'll turn up. It's just dark and foggy."

Mitchell called Frank's cell phone and it went straight to voicemail. "Where is this guy?" Mitchell asked.

Brett and Elda were now officially missing persons.

Even more people had shown up to help with the search. Several individuals had approached Mitchell to offer their sympathy and support.

Mitchell was polite but inside felt that every conversation was a waste of time – time that could be spent searching for his kids.

But the extra help had allowed them to expand their search. Sadly, despite the extensive coverage there were no sightings of the children or Karyn, and no new information.

Mitchell checked his phone. There were various notifications of people sending their love. Friends and family were posting on social media – no communication from Frank.

Nightfall made it difficult to see. The trees and forest floor seemed repetitive and endless.

Suddenly, Mitchell saw a large shape up ahead. He sprinted forward. There was a clearing ahead and inside it was a farmhouse! Mitchell slowed his pace and looked behind to see Detective Ernest jogging over.

The farm looked abandoned. They knocked on the front door. No answer. They knocked again. It looked like no one had been there for a long time.

Mitchell opened the door and then looked at the detective for approval. Ernest shrugged. They walked in and shined their flashlights throughout the dilapidated farmhouse. There were abandoned stalls and it smelled wretched. Above was a loft, presumably used to store hay in the past. They searched the farmhouse thoroughly for about ten minutes, eventually joined by a couple others from the search party, and found no one. There was no evidence the children had been there.

They stepped outside. "Are there any other houses or buildings out here?" Mitchell asked the detective. "I mean, maybe they're sleeping inside someplace or something."

"There's not much in the forest. Some farms, buildings and cabins but we think that Karyn went this way to escape being discovered so it's doubtful that she's stopping anywhere between here and the next town. I have officers checking all nearby towns, suburbs and cities. Anyways, we will definitely check out properties we come across, but in my opinion Karyn is avoiding them and making a run for the next town."

Mitchell leaned against a tree and thought about where his children might be. On top of everything, Frank was nowhere to be found. Mitchell steeled himself, took a deep breath and headed toward the detective to resume the search.

Surrounded in darkness the search party pressed on deeper into the vast, pitch-black woods – the woods that border hell.

Chapter 32

Brett fiddled with the vent cover and pulled it off. He climbed out and hopped down onto a heavy filing cabinet. There were a couple chairs in the room, including one large, cushioned chair. Brett lifted Elda down and she ran over to the soft chair. She decided to continue her earlier-interrupted nap.

Brett rushed over to the folder with his name on it and set the vent cover down. He opened the folder. There was a note scrawled and signed by Dr. Abscheulich:

Patient is a violet psychotic. Authority complex.

Refusal to reform. Must render subject docile.

Recommended treatment: Full physical incapacitation via cerebral surgery.

Brett shoved the note into his pocket. Under the note was a picture of Brett with his name written on the back. "I don't even want to know how they got this," Brett said to himself.

He then saw a shadow behind one of the cabinets. He walked toward it and stopped a few feet away. The shadow was a ghostly mist-like substance. It was that figure again! "Who are you? What are you?" The figure had a blurred face and stared right at him. Brett decided enough was enough. He charged at it and . . . ran right through it! He turned around and it was gone. Brett looked all over the room. There was no one in sight.

"Why am I seeing things?" Brett wondered to himself. "Who is this transparent, grey figure following me?"

Brett decided to look through the cabinets. He couldn't find his mother's folder under "Slinger." So, he thought for a moment and checked under her maiden name. Success! It was filed under Karyn Aargon. "That's weird," Brett thought. "Why did they use her maiden name?"

Something caught his eye. Directly before Karyn's folder was a file titled Clara Aargon. Aargon was the same last name as his mother's maiden name and Clara was the same first name as the woman that had been helping them . . .

He sat down and poured through the file. Reading page after page of data. What he found bewildered him.

Clara Aargon was institutionalized in 1950. Apparently she had upset an important family. She was pregnant at the time and ended up giving birth to a baby boy named George Aargon in the institution.

Brett stopped breathing. George was the name of his grandfather on his mother's side – George Aargon. Per the file, George was put up for adoption and Clara never saw him again after birth.

"What the hell?" Brett thought. "Grandpa George was adopted! He told us that he was put up for adoption after birth and that his biological mother had died in a mental institution. He said that she had named him George and that his foster parents had chosen to let him keep his full birth name in honor of his mother's passing. This can't be happening . . ."

He kept reading. Clara had been prescribed several psychotropic drugs and was operated on throughout her stay in the asylum. Electric shocks also had been performed on her. There were several notes in her folder that indicated she had tried to escape the facility on multiple occasions. She was an isolated patient that avoided social contact. The last note in the folder was dated 1952 . . .

Something fell to the floor. It was a picture. On the back of it was written Clara Aargon, 1950. Brett slowly turned over the photo. It was the same Clara that Brett and Elda had been talking to!

Brett fell backward in astonishment. His hand knocked a lamp off a table behind him. Crash!

"Elda!" Brett urged. "We need to get back into the ventilation shaft now." Elda blinked her eyes open. Brett ran over to her and picked her up. She stretched and let out a loud sigh. He lifted her into the shaft. She started to talk but Brett told her to be quiet. He could her people approaching the office. His stupidity had attracted their attention.

He began climbing into the shaft himself but realized he had left the vent cover on the table. He couldn't leave it there. Brett headed back to the table, grabbed the cover and bolted toward the shaft. He heard people at the door. He had no choice, he had to save Elda. He threw the map at her. "Elda, the bad guys are here," he said. "I need you to keep being brave. Please hide here. I'll come right back for you." Elda started to argue but Brett put the vent cover in place just as the door opened. Brett shushed Elda and she backed deeper into the shaft out of fear.

The staff that had been meeting in the next room entered. Brett prepared to fight but felt two darts pierce his body. One in the stomach and one in his right thigh. Brett fell to the floor. He prayed to god that Elda would keep silent and get away.

Drugs overwhelmed Brett's consciousness again and he slipped away into the dark.

Chapter 33

The path that Frank had been following had disappeared. He was lost in the forest. He continued walking forward in a straight line, using his flashlight to see.

There was no one around and it was very dark. Frank was intent on finding Brett and Elda. He had known them their whole life. Birthdays, barbecues, you name it. Frank's wife, Shelly, passed away from cancer about five years back. They never had any children. Mitchell had helped him through the tragedy.

Since Shelly's death, Frank spent more time around the Slinger family. To him, they were family. He was determined to locate them.

He had never got along with Karyn. He couldn't remember how many times he had advised Mitchell to stay away from her. He had had countless run-ins with her and bad experiences that had led him to the determination that it was best to stay away from her.

His flashlight began flickering. "Really?" Frank thought. Up ahead Frank noticed a large shape. He stopped walking and squinted. He shined the flickering flashlight in front of himself. Through the darkness and fog he made out a tall fence. His heart started beating faster.

"Karyn and the kids might be here!" Frank said to himself in excitement.

He walked up to the fence. His flashlight no longer worked. He looked through the bars of the fence and saw a massive hospital. There were large double-doors in front with men standing guard. The windows around the entrance shone light.

Frank yelled, "Hello!" He made his way over to a tall gate. He waved his arms and kept yelling at the men. He tried to open the gate but it was chained shut.

A large man walked toward the gate. "Who are you?" he asked Frank.

"I'm searching for a woman and two children," Frank answered. "They've gone missing."

"Who's with you?" the man asked in response.

"Why does that matter?" Frank snapped back. "I'm here alone."

The man snorted and unlocked the gate. "Welcome to Leiden Asylum."

"Did a blonde woman arrive here within the last day with a teenager and a little girl?"

"I don't know. I'll bring you to the doctor. He knows everything that happens here."

Frank followed the man into the asylum. It appeared to be quite an old building. Despite how late it was, there were staff and patients wandering about. No one was talking. Frank could feel stares.

"Wait here," the large orderly directed.

Frank stood in a reception area. He looked around. He noticed an aged calendar on the wall. It was dated 1952. Decades old.

Frank waited for about five minutes and the orderly returned. "I'm sorry," he said, "but Karyn and her kids aren't here."

Frank froze. He had never mentioned Karyn's name.

A look of recognition dawned on the orderly's face. He realized he had slipped up. He dove at Frank. Frank moved to the side and punched the orderly in the back of the head. The orderly crashed face first into the reception desk and collapsed on the floor.

Due to years of strenuous construction work under his belt, Frank was a large, strong man.

"They're here!" Frank said to himself.

Chapter 34

Brett awoke and found himself back in Dr. Abscheulich's office.

He felt slightly woozy but had pieced it together. The folder he read on Clara was saying that she, the woman he'd been working with to escape, was his great-grandmother! Supposedly Grandpa George was born in this institution. Brett thought, "This isn't possible. Clara is in her twenties. It's got to be some kind of trick or coincidence."

Brett was sitting on a couch and noticed that he wasn't strapped down. The room came into focus. Several feet in front of him, Karyn was strapped to a chair. And sitting at the main desk was Dr. Abscheulich. He held a pistol in his hand.

Brett tried to stand and the doctor trained the gun on Brett's mother. Brett sat abruptly.

"Stay seated, boy," the doctor ordered, "or I shall end your mother."

Karyn's head hung downwards. Her chin rested above her chest. Drool trailed down her cheek and her eyes were half-shut. She looked like a vegetable.

She was linked to an odd-looking machine. The machine was massive and it had a large dial that displayed waves of electricity. Lined along the bottom of it were hundreds of small switches. There were cords attached to Karyn's body that connected her to the strange apparatus.

"What did you do to her?" Brett asked.

"She's cured!" Dr. Abscheulich pronounced. "Karyn shall no longer exhibit psychotic tendencies."

Brett addressed his mother. "Mom?" No response.

"It appears you were discovered in our folder room," the doctor said. "Reviewing patient files. Have you figured it out yet?"

Brett remained silent. His mind was racing on how to get his mother and himself out of this situation. She looked terrible.

"Why are most of the patient files dated from the 1950s and earlier?" the doctor asked. "Why haven't you ever heard of this place? And more importantly, why do Clara and Karyn have the same last name?" Brett didn't respond. He wanted the doctor to keep talking. Partly so Brett could keep thinking, figuring out how to escape, but also because he was interested in hearing what the doctor had to say.

"Haven't you wondered why most of the people here look old-fashioned to you?" the doctor continued. "I figure I might as well tell you. Considering in short order I'll be forcing you into a catatonic state and after that, I will kill you."

Brett blinked.

"You see, in 1952, I received notification that the government was going to shut down my asylum. Apparently there had been too many complaints. All fallacious, of course. Fortuitously, I had been working on a special project for several years prior. I found that you could trap the life force of people. It's like draining electricity from a battery." The doctor pointed to the large device that Karyn was strapped to. "My machine holds the key to immortality. Life as a phantom. And the more life force I have, the more solid I can become."

Brett was confused.

"So, when I heard that they were going to shut us down, I gathered up all the staff and patients. I killed them all. How else do you think I've trapped all these ghosts here? Yes, ghosts. I stole their energy and used it to perpetuate everyone, including myself. The research had to go on, for the good of mankind of course. As years passed, I lured new souls in and, well, 'recharged' you could say."

Brett tensed up on the couch, hoping the doctor would finish his nonsensical babble.

"You see, I control which of my staff and patients are present. Their life is ensnared in my machine." The doctor again indicated the machine that Karyn was attached to. "I have an energy reserve that I use to project the forms of myself and others. When someone experiences pain or better yet, dies, my machine captures their vitality."

"I don't understand anything you're saying," Brett said.

"I don't expect a feeble-minded teenager like you to understand. Within the walls of this hospital is the answer to continued life after death. The machine is that answer. Which brings me to you. The only people who are really alive here are you, your sister and Karyn. I was able to draw you here because of the connection to your great-grandmother, Clara. Karyn's simple mind was easily manipulated."

Brett looked over to Karyn again. She hadn't moved once since he arrived.

"Taking your souls will provide me with adequate power to finally ensure I can leave the walls of this place. I've been saving up energy for years."

Brett's mouth was open. This doctor was more insane than he had thought! "Wait," Brett said, "you're telling me you expect me to believe that you're ghosts?"

"Well," the doctor said, "to live in the physical world, you must follow the rules of the physical world. How else do you think you can see us, touch us and even attack us? To exist, we are required to be seen. I utilized pilfered vitality to accomplish this."

"Sorry, man, but I've killed more than one person in self-defense since I've been here. You can't kill ghosts."

"Oh, none of them are dead. You'll see."

Brett rolled his eyes and said, "I don't believe any of this. There are so many holes in your story."

"Believe what you'd like. With your mother's life, I'll be one step closer to my goal. Every person that dies in Leiden Asylum adds power to my machine. Ideally, they're hardwired directly into it, as your mother is now. But I designed it to pull in all departing energy in this building."

With that, the doctor stood up and began walking toward Karyn.

Brett watched in horror and jumped up. Karyn slowly lifted her head and looked at him. "I am sorry, Brett. I love you. Tell your sister I love her forever too. I'm sorry." Bam!

Blood spattered onto Brett's face. He stumbled backward into the couch. The doctor had shot Karyn.

The machine began whirring. A bright blue light projected from the dial. It appeared to be shining with abundant electricity.

Brett sat on the couch in complete shock, crying.

Chapter 35

Frank heard a gunshot. He ran toward the sound. He was in a large room with a staircase. The sound had come from the office at the top of the stairs. A couple nurses stared at him and then yelled, "Sir, you can't be in here!"

Frank ignored them and ran to the top of the stairs. He kicked the iron door in and saw a terrible sight. Karyn was lying in a pool of blood on the floor, apparently deceased.

Brett was on a sofa sobbing and there was a doctor standing nearby. The doctor had a gun and was pointing it right at Frank. Frank stood in the doorway, frozen. He noticed a small table with a couple books on it next to himself.

"Who are you?" the doctor inquired.

Frank thought quickly and grabbed a heavy book. He threw it at the doctor and there was a gunshot. Years of playing football had paid off. The book smashed into the doctor's face and the shot missed Frank – a hole gaped in the wall behind him. The doctor fell into a heap on the ground. Frank ran over and picked up the pistol.

Brett got to his feet and walked over to Karyn's body. She lay on the floor, eyes still open and she wasn't breathing. It was a hideous sight. Brett forced himself to check her pulse – nothing. She was ice cold. There were so many things he had never gotten to say to her. He couldn't believe she was gone . . .

"We can definitely ensure you have time for mourning, but now is not the time," Frank said. "We need to get out of here right this second." Two nurses were carefully walking up the stairs toward Dr. Abscheulich's office.

"No," Brett said firmly. "Give me the gun."

"Brett, we don't have time –"

"Frank. Give me the damn gun."

Frank hesitantly handed the gun to Brett. Frank then slammed the office door and locked it.

Brett walked over to the doctor, who was sprawled out on the floor by the desk. For the first time, the formidable king of hell looked powerless as he lay unconscious on the floor. All the evil operations and destruction that took place at Leiden Asylum traced down to one corrupt soul, and Brett now held the devil's life in his hands.

Brett pressed the pistol against the doctor's temple. Frank yelled, "Brett, don't!" Brett kept the gun in place and pushed it harder against the side of Dr. Abscheulich's head. Turning to look at Frank, Brett said, "He tortured my mother and then put a bullet in her head. He's lucky I'm ending it quick."

Frank moved toward Brett and Brett pulled the trigger. Bam! Dr. Abscheulich met the same fate as Karyn.

Frank was stunned. He reached Brett and looked down. The doctor was deceased. Frank grabbed Brett's arm and tugged. "Let's go, man. Your dad is looking for you."

Brett ran with Frank down the stairs. There were a couple nurses in their path. Brett shoved past them.

They ran toward the front doors and there was a large group of institution staff blocking it. Brett noticed a large figure standing far off to the right. He looked; it was Masheck! How was that possible?

Brett heard a squeal, "Bro bro!" It was Elda. The sound came from a nearby ventilation shaft.

Frank looked at Brett. "Find another way out and get your sister out of here. I'll handle these guys."

"No -" Brett started.

Frank shoved Brett away and yelled, "Get Elda to safety, now!"

Brett complied and ran down a nearby hallway. He found a vent cover and tore it off. Elda scrambled toward him and they hugged. Brett climbed in and they started crawling through the shaft toward the outside vent.

"How did you find your way over here?" Brett asked Elda.

"It was like a video game!" she said. "I followed the map!" Brett was extremely impressed and proud of Elda for figuring it out. He told her that she did an excellent job and then asked her to be silent.

A gun fired several times and there was yelling. Through a vent Brett saw a couple staff sprawled across the floor. Frank was fighting off staff and Masheck was aggressively walking toward him.

Brett and Elda kept crawling, following the map, and reached the exit vent. Brett peered through and saw that the outside gate was open! Someone must've forgotten to lock it after Frank entered. But there were nearly ten different orderlies in the yard. They'd never get past them.

Suddenly Brett saw smoke. There was a fire inside the institution. All the staff in the yard ran inside the building to see what was happening. This was their chance!

Brett kicked the vent cover off and hopped onto the grass. He had Elda climb onto his back and he ran.

He looked back and saw Frank lying on the floor. Frank's neck was twisted in an unnatural direction. He was dead. Masheck stood with his back turned, wringing his hands. It looked like he had broken Frank's neck.

Brett's heart wrenched. He wanted to go back so badly to help Frank somehow but he couldn't risk Elda's safety. He pressed on, carrying his sister.

He looked back again and standing in front of Dr. Abscheulich's office, with a fire roaring behind her, Brett saw Clara. Apparently she had engaged in arson as a diversion.

Tears were in Brett's eyes as he ran through the gate. His mother was deceased. Frank had also died, protecting him. Clara had distracted everyone with a fire. They were escaping. It was all too much.

They reached the edge of the forest. They were surrounded in darkness. Elda was terrified and kept asking, "What's happening?" Brett looked back one last time. Masheck had one of his oversized hands wrapped around Clara's face. No one had noticed them and they weren't being followed. Staff and patients were clamoring and moving around in confusion.

"It's okay, sis'," Brett said as he set Elda down. "We are going to see Dad."

"Where's Mommy?" Elda asked. Brett sniffled and didn't answer. They held hands and walked into the trees together.

Chapter 36

It was late now. About half of the people involved in the search had headed home, with promises of resuming tomorrow.

Mitchell trudged along, next to the detective.

There was suddenly a yell! Someone further down the line was shouting. Mitchell and Ernest ran toward the noise. They heard, "We found them!"

Mitchell nearly fell over with surprise and sprinted. He then saw Brett and Elda huddled together by a member of the search party. Tears of joy burst from Mitchell's eyes. He couldn't believe it!

"Daddy!" Elda screamed. He hugged both children tightly.

"Dad," Brett said, "there's so much I need to tell you."

"Please," Mitchell responded, "let's get you guys home. Safe and warm. You need rest. You can tell me all about it later."

The combination of sleep-deprivation, malnourishment, drugs, stress, abuse and the hell he'd witnessed left Brett too weak to argue. Mitchell hugged the kids again and Brett passed out.

Part of the search team was a pair of medics that drove an ambulance. "We need medical attention over here!" an officer yelled.

The two medics ran over. "It looks like he's dehydrated. He needs liquids, food and rest. We are going to transport him to the hospital."

"Elda," Mitchell said, "where is Mommy?"

"I don't know, Daddy," Elda said.

"And Uncle Frank? Have you seen him?"

"No, Daddy."

Mitchell stood up. He reached down and picked up Elda to carry her. One of the police officers, a big guy, lifted Brett up and placed him over his shoulder.

After a little over twenty-four hours of anguish, the family was finally headed home – one member short.

Chapter 37

Shortly after Brett and Elda were found, Karyn and Frank's bodies were discovered. Police located the corpses in an old, shut-down institution called Leiden Asylum.

The search team found the asylum abandoned. A recent fire had been set, badly burning Karyn's body and damaging some of the property. The police determined that Karyn had been shot and that Frank's neck had been broken somehow.

The search team also found supplies of psychotropic drugs and several recently-used machines, including a strange, active box with a display monitor. Not knowing what it was or who it belonged to, they left it there. They also found Karyn's hair on an electroshock device – it appeared that people had been in the sanitarium recently.

Leiden Asylum had been closed in the 1950s following a series of complaints and a terrible tragedy that occurred. Records from that time reported that the head doctor, Luitpold Abscheulich, had led a mass murder of all staff and patients. He had gathered everyone up in a large hall and ended them with poisonous gas. He had included himself in the extermination.

Brett and Elda now lived with Mitchell. Mitchell owned a successful accounting firm and held a realtor's license. Brett had convinced him to move them all to a new city.

Mitchell had handled the accounting for Frank's construction company. They also had an ongoing concern wherein Mitchell would sell houses and Frank would renovate them. The loss of Frank had caused some significant changes in Mitchell's professional operating basis.

The months following the death of Frank and Karyn were hard on everyone. The children had lost a parent and been through hell. Mitchell had had his best friend and his ex-wife taken from him.

The family was, for the most part, back on their feet again. Mitchell had his company rolling and Elda was in first grade now. Brett wasn't attending school. He was spending most of his time in his room, alone.

One of the most annoying things the family had to deal with was constant media attention following the incident. Moving to a new city helped but there were still calls, emails, social media posts . . . As though the homicides weren't difficult enough, reporters kept it stirred up.

The worst thing was that the prime murder suspect was Brett.

Chapter 38

Mitchell, Brett and a lawyer arrived at the police station. The lawyer was from a major firm in the area – her name was Wendie.

"Brett," Wendie said, "we are only here as a courtesy to the police. You wanted to come, against my advice I might add. You are not formally being charged with anything, you're a minor and they have nothing on you. So, be calm and let's wrap this up quickly."

Brett and Wendie entered the interrogation room. Mitchell noticed Detective Ernest walking over and stayed back for a moment.

"Hey, Mitchell," the detective said, holding a coffee in his right hand.

"Hi, Detective," Mitchell responded with no trace of a smile on his face. "Is this really necessary?"

"He's our only suspect," Ernest said. "Hey, I'm not going to take it easy on him in there. I've got to do my job."

"Really? This is totally absurd. I thought what we had been through mattered. You helped me find them! And for

Christ's sake, their mother just died and Frank and —" Mitchell didn't realize it but he was yelling at this point.

"Stop," the detective interrupted forcefully. "Like I said, I've got a job to do." With that, Detective Ernest pushed past Mitchell and entered the interrogation room.

Mitchell followed after, steamed from the altercation. He joined Brett, Wendie and Ernest at a cold, metal table.

"Listen, Brett," the detective began, "I know you say you didn't do it but there are some things that aren't adding up. First off, you and Elda were the only people present at the time of Frank and Karyn's death. There aren't any fingerprints, hair samples; nothing indicating anyone else was in that asylum. And we all know that Elda didn't do it. Second of all, Karyn's time of death is thirty minutes before Frank's and we can't find any legitimate motive that he would have to shoot and then burn her. Another odd factor is that the autopsy revealed that Karyn underwent electroshock therapy while in the asylum — a test of one of the machines found there confirmed it had been recently used."

"Brett," the lawyer said, "I advise you not to respond to the detective during this interview."

The detective leaned in closer. "Your dad is insisting you didn't do this. And to be honest, we haven't found evidence that you did. The gun we found was badly burned and we couldn't get any fingerprints off it. It's also highly unlikely that you broke Frank's neck due to how much larger he is than you. But there are two factors that point the finger at you: 1. You know martial arts and 2. You had motive to kill

Karyn. We know she abused you, Brett. I understand that you may have gotten fed up and -"

Brett cut in, "This is ridiculous!" Brett's lawyer motioned for him to stop talking but he continued on. "I saw her shooter and I saw someone attack Frank. Just because you can't find evidence of that doesn't mean it didn't happen."

Mitchell interjected, "Brett, you don't have to say anything. Please listen to the lawyer."

"Dad, I can handle this," Brett replied. He looked at the detective and continued talking. "My mother was unstable for sure, but I didn't kill her! And Frank was a family friend. I cared about them both. I am innocent."

The detective looked thoughtfully at Brett, leaned back and responded, "Okay. Here's the deal. My job as a detective is to remain unbiased and follow the evidence. Like I said, there's no evidence that anyone else was with you guys at the asylum, and you have motive."

"That's not true. Even if you say that I had motive to kill Karyn, what motive would I have to murder Frank?"

"Maybe he witnessed you killing your mother."

"Well, that's not true because I didn't do it. Plus, how do you explain the drugs you found and recent usage of various machines? You think I smuggled in psychotropic medications and figured out how to operate complex machinery? Your case is full of holes. I can't believe that the same detective that helped find my sister and me is now trying to falsely accuse me of these crimes."

"Stop making this personal; I'm just doing my job and trying to gather the facts."

"How could this be more personal? You're accusing me of murder."

"Calm down, Brett. We haven't located anyone matching the descriptions you gave us for the killers. You're the only suspect and I need to determine whether or not you're guilty once and for all."

"Just because you're unable to catch criminals doesn't mean I'm the culprit."

"Well, Brett, how do explain that we found drugs in your system after you were rescued? Drugs were also discovered in Karyn's body during the autopsy."

"We were drugged by the men I described. Please, you've got to start listening to me."

The lawyer interjected, "This is going nowhere and the interrogation is over. My client was obviously assaulted and the real murderer or murderers have not been captured. Unless you can find actual evidence, detective, this slanderous conjecture will never make it to trial."

Chapter 39

I am Brett and this was my story.

I wrote this book to share my experience at Leiden Asylum – the institution that stole my mother, a close family friend and my great-grandmother from this world.

I now believe in ghosts. It is the only explanation for what I've been through.

I figure that destroying Dr. Abscheulich's machine is the key. I'm assuming that releasing the energy stores in the machine will erase the evil spirits and allow everyone to move on to whatever lays beyond this life. The good souls he's trapped, like Clara, deserve to be freed. Hasn't she been through more than enough already?

Based off what Dr. Abscheulich told me and what I've been able to piece together, the machine apparently had a switch for each trapped being. The doctor simply flipped the switch off or on to determine whether or not that ghost would be present. Masheck, Nurse Rieck, each of these people had a switch that either contained their energy or projected their ghost. Maybe there was even a switch for the doctor himself?

For whatever reason, Dr. Abscheulich had decided not to display the staff and patients of the sanitarium when the police arrived. To them, it was a dilapidated building with no one in it. The police didn't see the fully manned and operational asylum that I saw. Most likely the doctor turned everyone's "switch" off, and somehow hid himself, to avoid being exposed. But why didn't the doctor leave everyone in existence and just kill the police? All that I can figure is he didn't want to risk drawing further attention to the institution. He must have left Karyn and Frank's bodies where they were to match up with the story he knew I would tell the police. He also had to know I wouldn't mention ghosts.

These are my assumptions, anyway.

After the visit to the police station, it took a couple more weeks but I was finally cleared of all charges. I had no police record and my lawyer, Wendie, was expensive and experienced. During the investigation the detective discovered unsolved missing persons reports in the area. The drugs found on site and other factors indicated a high likelihood that others had been present at the institution. No one could prove any wrongdoing on my part. It was finally determined that to take my case to trial on potential motive alone wasn't going to fly.

I intentionally withheld any references to ghosts or dead people during the murder investigation. While I did describe Masheck and Dr. Abscheulich in detail to the police, I didn't mention their names and the fact they had been deceased for decades. I knew no one would believe me – no need in getting myself thrown in another mental institution!

While it was a relief to be off the hook, the stress of being a murder suspect was overwhelming – it was bad enough to lose loved ones. The detective eventually apologized to my father and me for the added strain and false accusations.

They never did find my mother's or Frank's killer. Their deaths have been written off as unsolved homicides.

We now live with my dad, Mitchell.

I have drifted out of touch with my friends. Lillian (my crush from school) and I haven't spoken in months.

People worry about me. Up until now, I've only shared my story with a few others. Most of them think I'm insane. Some believe that I suffered a mental breakdown through the loss of Frank and Karyn.

My dad is the only one that has shown any sign of belief in my story. I had to beg him to not go to Leiden Asylum. I'm sure he would be trapped and killed if he ventured there.

My dad has been wonderful. He's allowed me to take a break from school. I've spent the extra time writing and researching this book. It took me some time to piece everything together and I've attempted to remain as accurate as possible.

The problem with my story is that I have no proof. There are no other (living) witnesses, except Elda. But she was too young to realize what was happening.

I am constantly worried that Dr. Abscheulich, Nurse Rieck or someone else from that dreaded hellhole will come for me.

My dad has a connection in the book industry and I am sending this book off to the publisher tomorrow morning. As I sit in my room now, I still feel waves of sadness when I think about Karyn, Frank and Clara.

Elda and my dad are currently out at a movie. I stayed home because of how close I am to getting this published.

What was that? There's a movement in the corner of my room!

After months of no paranormal experiences, there's a mist forming into a human shape right before my eyes! It's the fogged form I saw back in the forest and at the asylum – a man with his back turned to me.

Suddenly, I can't speak and I can't breathe.

I am trying to talk but I can't force out the words. My throat feels dry and cracked.

The partially transparent phantom head is turning toward me. Finally, I can make out the ghost's face. I don't know why I hadn't figured it out before . . .

Dr. Abscheulich! The blurry figure had been the doctor all along! He is smiling, drifting toward me and -

THE END

Thank you for reading Suffer Asylum by Jack Carl Stanley!

Find out more at:

sufferasylum.com

facebook.com/sufferasylum

twitter.com/SufferAsylum

The author can be reached at:
jackstanleyportland@gmail.com

Buy additional copies of this book at Amazon.com.